Today's Truth

Terri D

www.AuthorTerriD.com

ISBN: 978-0-9831887-1-1
Library of Congress Control Number:

Interior & Cover Art:
www.WeReadLiteraryServices.com

Printed in the USA

Dedication

To my mother, Patricia Gadsden, thanks for always believing in me and encouraging me to never give up. Your positive attitude and outlook even when staring in the face of adversity was at times annoying ☺ but you taught me how to persevere. I love you and as I always say, when I grow up I want to be just like you. You are my hero and the wind beneath my wings.

Acknowledgments

I would like to thank God for all of the blessings he has given me. It's because of him that I am able to make it through all of the trials and tribulations of life. To my children Steven Antonio White, Jasmine Marjorie-Lynn Washington and Jennifer Marie Washington, my grandson Jaylen Clark Washington, I thank you all for giving me a reason to never settle and to keep pushing myself each and every day. To my family, Aunt Donna, Cousin Tonya, my sisters Tanya & Michelle thanks for your continued love and support. Thanks to my BFF Maria and Catherine for your continued love and support. To the members of my church home Imani African Christian Church, your encouragement and support has meant the world to me. Thanks to my biggest fan from my Chatham Hall family, Judy Duncan for helping decide on the title and for telling everyone how much you loved Yesterday's Lies. To my mentor/coach/friend Junnita, I know I drive you crazy sometimes with all my questions and requests but you still answer when I call. ☺ To everyone else that I have crossed paths with this past year at the various book festivals and events I have attended. I appreciate your support, advice and encouraging words. I would also like to give a special shout out to the authors of the All4One Facebook group for all of your support and advice over the past year. To the rest of my family, friends and readers thanks for your continued support. Now I want to know. Are you ready for the truth?

Prologue

Dear Journal,

It's after midnight, so I can officially start my new journal since I am now thirty years old today. WOW! I can't believe I'm actually thirty. Where has the time gone? As I do every year, I'm starting a new journal to chronicle the events of my life. I usually start with an introduction, and this time, I will start with a summary of the past decade since this is a milestone year. My name is Toni Dickerson. Wow, I still can't get used to my married name—Dickerson. Yes, I'm married, FINALLY. Darien and I met at work and married about six months ago. We now have a four-month-old son named Darien, Jr. but we call him Lil' Darien. We work for American Health Products; I'm a sales rep in Marketing, and he's a manager in Accounting. I love my job in Marketing and am in conflict about returning to work now that Lil' Darien is here.

The past year has been full of life changing events for my friends and me. My circle of friends, as I have referred to them over the past decade, include my best friend Jada, her husband David, Jr., who was killed this past year in a terrible car accident, and my long-lost love Benjamin. The four of us grew up together in Greenbelt, Maryland, attended the same high school, and then went to Penn State together. Things were great for the four of us until our senior year of college.

Benjamin and I had a bad fight and broke up for a couple of months at the end of the summer heading into our senior year.

1

During that time, we both started dating other people. I dated a guy named Vinny, or Vince as I later found out. A month after Benjamin and I reconciled, I discovered I was pregnant. Benjamin was favored for a first round pick in the NBA draft. I knew my pregnancy would be a distraction for him, and I wasn't sure whose baby I was carrying, his or Vinny's. An opportunity came up for a marketing internship in Chicago, so I jumped at the chance to take it. I needed some time to think about how to handle the pregnancy and establishing paternity.

As it turns out, Jada also became pregnant right about the same time, and she and David, Jr. made plans to marry right after graduation. Jada was also a marketing major, and David was graduating with a degree in sports medicine. Jada and David, Jr.'s plans for life after college were solid. Jada planned to pursue a career in marketing, and David's plan was to get a coaching position at a high school.

A few months into my internship in Chicago, I received a call from Jada that Benjamin had been hurt during practice for the playoffs. It was thought to be a career-ending injury. Benjamin was devastated and had fallen into a deep depression. He was not responding to anyone and asked to be left alone until he was ready to talk. Jada was calling to let me know that this included me, as well. I wasn't buying it at all. I tried calling and emailing him, but didn't receive any response. After a few days, I considered traveling back to Pennsylvania to see him in person. However, a quick glance in the mirror at my protruding belly quickly brought me back to reality. There was no way I was springing this pregnancy on him while he was going through this. So, I decided to give him some time.

Meanwhile, I would work on trying to contact Vinny to let him know about the pregnancy and that we would need a paternity test. Vinny and I only dated briefly, and I was not able to locate him. He attended a college in Pittsburgh, and obviously, the information he gave me was only partially true.

After the first month of not hearing from Benjamin and not getting any responses to my messages, I became depressed. After three months, I decided the best course of action was to put the baby up for adoption and move on with my life. I was scared and alone with no one to turn to. Jada's life was moving along just fine, while I was pregnant and alone, not knowing who had fathered my child. I asked myself how I got here. There was no answer.

My love, Benjamin, had disappeared from my life for seven long years without so much as a phone call, letter, or an email. Looking back over the past decade, I now realize I wasted seven good years of my life mourning the loss of Benjamin and trying to find that love I felt with him with so many Mr. Right Now's along the way.

After my internship in Chicago, I landed a full-time job with the same company in their Harrisburg, Pennsylvania office. Harrisburg is the capital of Pennsylvania, but it is a very small city compared to what I was used to growing up in suburban Maryland. I moved first, and Jada and David, Jr. followed within a year after they were both able to secure jobs here, also. Jada ended up working for the same company as me, and David got a coaching position for one of the local school districts.

I was in a deep state of depression for a long time. I know that Jada and David, Jr. moved here because they were concerned about me. It took me two years to halfway get over the loss of Benjamin, and once I did start dating again, I had a string of unfulfilling and emotionally abusive relationships. Jada was always there for me, trying to help pick up the pieces whenever I suffered another heartbreak.

Last year was a great year for me. I met my husband, Darien, and it's weird because it's like I knew as soon as we met that he was the one. Jada, of course, was skeptical because she says I always felt like the next guy was the one. Imagine her surprise when Darien did turn out to be the one. Just when things were going well for Darien and I, after seven years and out of the blue, Benjamin calls me one night. Calling me baby and telling me how much he missed me. To say I was in shock would be an understatement. Then, as if the shock of Benjamin coming back wasn't enough, BOOM! I found out I was pregnant. I was scared to death that Darien would reject me because he felt like I tried to trap him.

Right in the middle of all of this drama, Jada's husband David, Jr. was in a tragic car accident and died. All of my problems were put on hold because my girl needed me. The next bombshell was when we discovered that Vinny from my college days was actually Vince, my husband Darien's best friend. This means that the baby I gave up for adoption could be my husband's best friend's baby. Now, keep in mind that no one knew I had a baby and had given it up for adoption, not even Jada until just before David's accident.

I discovered Vinny was Vince while at Vince's wedding to Gina. This is actually the day that Darien proposed to me after I revealed my prior relationship to him about Vince and I. Vince and Gina are no longer together. Their marriage didn't even last a year, but that's a long story that won't be told here.

Over the past year, Benjamin has returned, and I now know the truth about his whereabouts. He was in jail serving time for a crime he did not commit. David held this truth from me all of these years. He died before I knew the truth, and to this day, Jada doesn't know her husband committed the crime that Benjamin did time for. On one hand, I am very angry with David, Jr. for keeping the truth from me, but on the other hand, I am happy with Darien. So, it really shouldn't matter where Benjamin was, right? Well, that's what I keep telling myself, but I sometimes can't help thinking what if.

It's getting late, so I'm going to close for the night. I have a big day ahead of me tomorrow as I celebrate turning 30. YUCK!

Chapter 1

Benjamin

While sitting in the airport waiting for the next announcement about my flight, I thought about why I agreed to this trip anyway. I was on my way to Chicago to meet with the attorney that Vince had hired to help us with the paternity case. Vince and I barely knew each other. We dated the same girl, Toni, back in college eight years ago. We both recently found out that she had gotten pregnant by one of us and had given the baby up for adoption. I sent Vince a text message telling him that I was delayed and to proceed with the meeting without me. He could fill me in once I got there, and then we could discuss the next course of action.

I had mixed emotions about this trip. Initially when I found out about the child Toni gave up, I wanted to pursue finding the child. After David's death, and finding out Toni had moved on and was in a relationship with someone else, I decided to focus on my future and let the past go. Things were going very well for me with the job David, Sr. had pulled some strings to get for me. Being an ex-con, I knew it wasn't going to be easy to get employment, but David, Sr. could always find a way around every technicality, except for the fact that he hadn't been able to keep me out of jail. I was grateful for the job opportunity because I loved being back in the sports industry. I would rather be playing or coaching, but being a recruiter has it benefits, also. I enjoyed traveling and discovering new talent, and helping to mold their future was very fulfilling.

In the eleven months that have passed since the funeral, I've had very little contact with Toni, and Jada still doesn't want anything to do with me. David, Sr. and I keep in touch from time to time. He's still trying to be protective of Jada and is adamant that he does not want her to know the truth. He wants his son's image to remain pristine in the eyes of his wife and children. It bothers me that he is so comfortable with such a big lie being out there, but he helped me land this job. Therefore, I'm not trying to make any waves with him right now. If things were different with Toni and I, then I might feel compelled to press the issue of getting the truth out.

In one of my lunch meetings with David, Sr., I learned that Toni actually got married and had a baby. At first, I was very angry. After all, she was supposed to be my wife. Then I realized how unfair it was to feel that way. She had been in the dark for over seven years about my whereabouts. She had no idea why I stopped calling her. I felt a sharp pain in my heart every time I thought about her being alone in Chicago having the baby and not knowing who the father was. It must have been horrible for her. The irony of the situation haunted me. I gave up seven years of my life so my best friend could be around to be a father to his child. Meanwhile, the love of my life gave up a child that could have been mine.

The anniversary of David's death was near, and it was proving to be a very difficult time for me. I missed my friend, but I was still hurt and angry that he did not pass my letters along to Toni. I knew deep in my heart she still loved me. I was confident she would have waited for me if she had known the truth. None of this mattered right now, though. Toni was married and had a child. She had moved on with her life, and I needed to do the same.

I wondered what I would do if it turned out I was the father of her child. Vince begged me to make this trip with him. He had hired a private detective to track down the child, and the process was easier than we both thought it would be. We found the child, a little boy who we believed belonged to one of us. Now we were in the process of getting the court to rule on a paternity test for us. Vince was on a mission to determine which of us was the father. I didn't really know him, so I had no idea what his sudden motivation was to find the child. Months had gone by with neither one of us doing anything about it. Then, a few months ago, I received a phone call from him telling me what his plans were and asking if I would agree to be tested if he found the child. I only agreed because I didn't think he would actually locate the child. As long as the child wasn't found, it did not seem real to me. It was something I could put in the back of my mind and not deal with. Now that the child has been found, I have to face reality.

I thought about my own childhood. My mother, who was a single parent, raised me and died when I was in Junior High School. Then I went to live with my best friend David, Jr. and his family. I never knew much about my father, and now that there's the possibility I might be a father to a child who did not know me, it made me remember how lost and alone I felt at times while growing up.

My mother was wonderful. She worked hard to make sure I had everything I needed and most of what I wanted. Even though we were not wealthy like David's family, my mother found a way to ensure I had the best. I remember times when my mother worked three jobs, two full-time and one part-time job. She was always so tired, but she never complained, and she never had a bad word to say about my father. She didn't have to, because the older I got, the more I understood about the situation. My father just didn't want to be bothered with the responsibility of being a parent. I remember as a young child thinking to myself that I would never leave my children fatherless like he did me.

When Toni and I were together back in college and she brought up the subject of having children, I always cringed. Sure, I wanted children, but I wanted them when I knew I would have the time to spend with them like children need and deserve. I was headed for a promising NBA career, and the last thing I wanted was to be on the road for weeks at a time and not be able to see and spend time with my children. I wonder if this might have been a factor in Toni's decision to keep her pregnancy from me all those years ago.

Every time I thought about Toni, I pictured her smooth caramel skin, bright smile with perfect white teeth, and those big beautiful brown eyes of hers. She had a smile that made my heart melt like butter on a hot summer day. The image of her always brought a smile to my face, but as quick as the smile formed, it disappeared. Those fond memories were always accompanied by heaviness in my chest that felt like the wind was being sucked out of my lungs.

"I have to move on with my life," I said aloud to myself, then looked around to see if anyone heard me talking to myself.

While I waited, I decided to check my voicemails at the office. I had one message, and while listening to it, I shook my head. The message was from Vince's wife, Gina, the reporter who had approached me at David's funeral. She had been leaving me messages for months, wanting to interview me. Initially, she expressed wanting to talk to me more about my connection to David. She said she wanted to do another story about his life to honor him, and since I gave the eulogy at his funeral, she wanted to interview me about our friendship. After I started my recruiting job, she contacted me to say she wanted to interview me to do a story on my background and how I came to be a recruiter. I kept dodging her calls because I felt she was fishing for some dirt on David, and I was not in the mood for any drama. In addition, I had mentioned her repeated phone calls to David, Sr. a few months ago, and he advised me not to speak to her. Obviously, he had the same concerns I did about her motives. I considered mentioning the annoying calls from his wife to Vince when I saw him, but thought better of it. I had a hunch things were not going very well for them right now, so I was just going to let it go.

After deleting the message, I stood up to walk towards the counter to check on my flight. As soon as I reached the counter, the agent announced we were about to start boarding soon. So, I sent Vince a quick text message to give him the update on my flight. Then I gathered my belongings and waited for the announcement about first-class passengers. Since I had been sitting in the terminal daydreaming for hours, I planned to use the time during the flight to catch up on some work I needed to do, which included reviewing the files of some potential recruits.

I must have been exhausted, because I ended up sleeping the entire way to Chicago. I sent Vince a text as soon as we landed to see if he was picking me up or if I needed to grab a cab. I headed towards baggage claim while waiting for his response. I retrieved my bag and checked my phone, but no response from Vince. So, I decided to get a cab and head to the hotel. I sent him a text letting him know my plan. I assumed he was still meeting with the attorney about the paternity test.

I made my way to the hotel, checked in, left a message at the front desk for Vince, and got settled in my room. Since I had not gotten any work done on the plane, I decided to review the files while waiting to hear from Vince. As soon as I took the files out of my briefcase and got settled in the chair, there was a light knock on the door.

I opened the door and greeted Vince, who I had only seen once before when he came down to meet with me about hiring the private investigator to look for the child. He looked a lot shorter than I remembered, but then again, since I was 6'5" everyone seemed short to me. Vince stood about 5'9" and had a dark chocolate complexion. He looked a little defeated. His face was shiny; he looked hot and sweaty like he had run a marathon and lost.

"Vince, good to see you again."

"Man, I'm not so sure about that. This is not how I want to be spending my time, if you know what I mean," he responded.

I simply nodded in agreement as we shook hands. I invited him in, and after he entered the room, he started telling me all about the meeting with the attorney.

"Well, here is what I found out today. The child Toni gave up is a boy whose name is Derrick. He's eight years old, of course." He paused for a brief moment to gauge my reaction.

When he saw I had none, but was sitting in silence waiting for him to continue, he finally went on.

"A couple had adopted him as an infant. They divorced two years ago and are still fighting over custody of him. The attorney said our timing was impeccable. The judge, who was a week away from rendering his decision on custody, is now agreeing to hear our case requesting a test to determine paternity."

I stood up and started pacing back and forth. Vince stopped talking again, waiting for me to speak.

Finally, I said, "Wow, are you serious about us just being in the nick of time, man? That's crazy."

He nodded. "Yes, I'm serious. We have a private hearing in the judge's chambers tomorrow morning. He wants to hear from both of us regarding what our plans will be for Derrick if one of us is in fact his biological father."

I stopped pacing, sat back down, and put my head in my hands. All of this was happening so fast. Since I never thought Vince would locate the child, I never imagined I would have to stand before a judge and discuss what my plans would be if I was the child's father. Vince interrupted my private thoughts.

"Benjamin, honestly, I'm worried neither of us will make a good impression on the judge."

"Why do you say that?" I was a little confused by his last comment.

Now he stood up and started pacing back and forth. Finally, he said, "Well, I'm worried because I'm having issues with Gina. We haven't been married a year, and we're already separated…and well, I don't know any details or anything, but I heard that—"

I cut him off before he could finish.

"You heard that I had been in jail for the past seven years."

He simply nodded his head in agreement.

"Yes, I'm concerned about how that will look," I told him. "But I'm also a little worried about the fact that my job requires me to travel so frequently. I don't have a good support system around me to assist with taking care of a child."

Vince was right; neither of us looked like a good choice. Vince sat back down and looked at me.

"Benjamin, I have thought long and hard about this entire situation, and I've decided if I'm Derrick's father, I'm going for full custody."

"I applaud you, man, but I'm not sure that will the best choice for me. I'm just going to pray about it, sleep on it, and make my final decision in the morning."

"I can understand your position, man, but my mind is made up," he told me. "So did you get anything to eat yet? We could grab a bite to eat together and continue this conversation."

"Nah, I really can't. I'm tired from my trip, and I really have some work to do."

Although I did have work to do, I really just didn't want to share a meal with Vince. I didn't know him very well and was not in the mood for chitchat over dinner.

Vince stood up and headed towards the door. "I understand," he turned and said. "Let's meet in the lobby in the morning around nine o'clock, and we can share a cab to the courthouse."

I walked over to where he stood. "Yes, that sounds like a good plan." I turned the knob and pulled the door open. "I'll see you in the morning, man. Have a good evening."

As Vince walked out the door and headed down the hallway towards the elevator, he said, "Yep, you too, man. See you in the morning."

After Vince left, I laid back on the bed and stared at the ceiling for the longest time. I closed my eyes, picturing Toni and what she looked like all those years ago. I tried to remember what she looked like when she left for her internship. I was searching my memory for any sign that something was different. Thinking back, I do recall that she was acting a little strange. The sudden internship seemed a little odd, but I was so wrapped up in my own world that I did not pay attention. Knowing what I do now, I wish I had paid more attention.

I also thought about the time I spent in jail for my friend David, Jr. At the time, the decision I made seemed like the noble thing to do. I loved David, Jr. and always felt indebted to him and his father because of how they took me in after my mother died. When my mother got sick, she worried about me ending up on the street like some of my cousins and uncles. When David and I became friends—even though her friends and cousins chastised her about letting me run around with the little white boy in the neighborhood—she stood her ground and allowed me to spend as much time as I wanted with David. I never knew the details of how I ended up with the Wrights after mom died. I just know that David, Sr. took me to my house after the funeral and told me to pack my things because I was coming to live with them. Now my decision to stand in for David, Jr. would haunt me for the rest of my life. I knew the court would not be very receptive to giving a child to someone with a record. Part of me felt like finding out I was the father but not being granted custody would be worse than not knowing at all.

I was prepared to fight for my rights if the child was in fact mine. I had discussed it with David, Sr., and he offered to provide whatever legal assistance he could. I was not sure I would seek full custody, but I wanted Derrick to know I was his father and be able to spend time with him. Deep down, I wondered if finding out that we had a son together would change Toni's mind about getting back together with me. I had to remind myself that the past is done; I need to focus on the here and now. Look ahead, not back.

I got up and went over to the desk to log in and check my emails. As I scrolled down the messages, some of them spam, I did a double-take at one particular email address. I clicked to open it and was pleasantly surprised to see it was a message from Toni. It read:

Dear Benjamin,
        I hope this message finds you doing well. I wanted to check to see if you planned to come up to visit David's gravesite

next week. Jada and I are going to have a little gathering at her house on Saturday, and if you were going to be around, you could certainly join us. It would be nice for you to come since you and David, Jr. were so close.

Also, I heard you were working with Vince to find the child I gave up. I wanted to let you know that if you find the child and you are in fact the father, we should really sit down and talk about what that means for all of us. I am sure you've heard that I'm married now and have a son. Any decisions about my child would need to be discussed with my husband, also. I am sure you understand.

I'm not angry or mad. I just don't want any drama. Things are going well so far with my husband, and I do not want to do anything to upset my marriage. I do hope you understand my position. I hope you're not doing all of this in an attempt to have us reconcile. Even though I now understand where you were and why, I cannot reconcile with you. Our time has passed; it is time for us both to move on. We can remain friends, but anything more than friends is not going to happen.

Let me know as soon as you can about next weekend so I can let Jada know.
~Toni

Chapter 2

Vince

I sat in my hotel room with the TV on. I wasn't really watching it, but needed some noise to distract my thoughts, which were all over the place. I was still feeling anxious after the meeting with the attorney and from thinking about the meeting with the judge scheduled for the next day. I was still dealing with drama with Gina, and this trip was a perfect excuse to get away for some time to myself. I wished I could call my boy Darien to talk to him. Things just hadn't been the same between us since we discovered his wife used to be my girlfriend. Even though it was over eight years ago and we only dated briefly, I understood how he felt. If things were reversed, I would be uncomfortable, also.

This subject regarding the baby Toni gave up was very uncomfortable for both of us, so I decided against calling him. In the beginning, I think we both thought we could handle it, but as time passed and when I decided to pursue finding the child, Darien was less than thrilled about it. I tried to let it go, but I couldn't ignore the fact that there was a child out there somewhere who might belong to me. I had to know. So, here I sit alone in my room thinking about what to say to the judge. I knew if the child were mine, things would get even worse between Darien and I. There's no doubt in my mind I would want to be in Derrick's life if he turns out to be mine.

The thought of tomorrow morning's meeting made me nervous because it would bring me one step closer to knowing the truth. My attorney and I had already briefly discussed me seeking full custody, and he told me if I wanted to pursue custody, I could since I had never officially given up my paternal rights to the child. I had mixed emotions about all of this. On one hand, if Derrick were my son, I wanted to fight to get him. On the other hand, Derrick, who was already eight years old, didn't know me, and if I knew he was in a stable home, I might be able to walk away, not wanting to disrupt his life. However, when I found out he was in the middle of a custody battle with his adopted parents, I felt more compelled to take action. I hadn't completely determined how being with me, a single father who he just met, could be any better than being with one of his adopted parents who had raised him his entire life. I needed to come up with a convincing argument and quick before the meeting tomorrow.

The attorney tried to calm me down by telling me the judge just wanted to have an informal conversation with Benjamin and me about what our intentions were after paternity was established. My attorney also felt the judge was interested in the relationship between Benjamin and Toni, as well as me. I really tried to convince Toni to participate in this process, but she was adamant that she wanted to leave the past in the past. I think it was more a matter of Darien not being able to handle it. Whatever the reason, it would just be Benjamin and me appearing before the judge. We both had to plead our cases for why we wanted a paternity test performed on Derrick and what we would do if we found out we were the father.

As crazy as it was for me to be thinking about Gina, I was. I wished things could be different and she could be here by my side through all of this. Then again, would I even be here if things were different between Gina and me?

I had to decide how to explain my separation from my wife, who I married less than a year ago. I didn't want to get into a lengthy discussion about Gina because I knew I would become angry, and I didn't need the judge seeing that side of me right now. Even though if I explained the entire story to him, I'm sure he would understand my anger. I shook my head, thinking between Benjamin and me, the judge would have a field day with us. Two single men, one with a record and the other with relationship issues trying to seek custody of an eight-year-old boy. How crazy is that?

I was a little disappointed that Benjamin didn't want to go to dinner tonight. I really wanted to get to know him a little better. When Gina and I were still together, she always talked about trying to interview him to finish her story on David Wright. She had done a piece on him a couple of years ago. After his tragic death, she attended the funeral, where Benjamin gave the eulogy. She had planned to do a follow-up story on David's life and wanted to interview Benjamin about their connection. I wasn't trying to do Gina's work for her, but I was interested in their connection, also. Clearly, they were from very different backgrounds. From what Gina had gathered from her initial interview with him, David, Jr. was from an affluent family, while Benjamin was just a regular guy. Not really sure what the common thread was there, but I was intrigued. Gina also found it odd that during the interview when she talked to him about people who had an influence on his life and career, he never mentioned Benjamin. Then he showed up at the funeral, is introduced as his best friend, and delivered the eulogy. I was curious about his criminal record that Darien had mentioned to me in passing.

I had been lying around thinking about everything for what felt like hours. I checked the clock, and it was only nine. So, I decided to head downstairs to the restaurant to get a bite to eat. I could have ordered room service, but I wanted to get out and mingle a bit.

After changing my shirt, I headed downstairs and requested a table near the piano so I could enjoy the entertainment. I had already checked out who was there and saw no potential dinner companions, so I would be eating and listening to music alone.

As I listened to the piano player, someone approached him, and I couldn't believe my eyes. It was Greg, an old classmate from

17

college. Apparently, he knew the piano player and was waiting for an opportunity to talk to him. I got up and headed over towards Greg to say hello. I wondered if he would remember me. He looked exactly the same as he did the last time I saw him. At that moment, I made a mental note to rejoin the gym because I knew I had gained at least twenty pounds since college. As I approached him, he turned and recognized me.

"Vincent Smith, what in the world brings you to town?"

We shook hands and did the half-hug man thing.

"Greg, if I told you, you wouldn't believe me anyway," I replied.

He laughed and said, "Yep, with you, man, I can only imagine. Seriously, though, are you here on business or a pleasure trip?"

I thought about his comment for a minute, but couldn't be mad or offended at his remark because I was always into something when I was in college.

Finally, I responded, "I'm here on personal business, but enough about me. What's been going on with you? Are you still writing music?" He motioned for me to step aside so we could talk in private.

"Yes, I'm writing music, and I believe I've just gotten my big break," he told me.

"Wow, man, that is wonderful! So who are you working with?"

Greg shook his head. "It's not a done deal yet, so I can't get into the details, but what's going on with you? Are you still writing, too?"

"Actually, I am. I've been doing commercials and working with a few small groups back home."

The piano player stopped playing and started walking in our direction. Greg turned towards him and introduced us. His name was Jeremy, and it turns out he was actually a student of Greg's.

Greg and I exchanged information, and he promised to be in touch as soon as his deal was official. Then I returned to my table just as my food arrived. I was so glad I had come downstairs instead of ordering room service. Running into Greg could be the break I was looking for. I needed something to jump-start my career. Especially since I might be a father.

I ate my meal and enjoyed listening to Jeremy play. He was very talented and had such an intense expression on his face when he played. I could tell music was his passion, and I thought about why I never considered teaching music, even if just as a side gig and nothing formal. When I thought about the possibility of being able to work with Greg or starting a little studio where I worked teaching kids how to play, I grew very excited. So, I headed back to my room to write down some of my ideas and prepare for the meeting in the morning.

Chapter 3

Benjamin

After reading Toni's email last night, I decided not to respond right away. I re-read it several times trying to look for any evidence that she still loved and wanted me. She did say it would be nice to see me. *Hmm, I wonder if that has any hidden meaning behind it.*

In my mind, I knew it was over and I needed to let it go, but my heart still longed for the connection that Toni and I once shared. The entire time I was in prison I thought about her every day. I imagined she thought of me, too, and would be waiting for me the day I was released.

As I got ready to meet Vince, I reminisced back to the night when I first called her. Her response to my call surprised me. I remember how angry I felt after realizing she had no idea where I had been. It's horrible to say now since he's dead, but I wanted to kill David for not giving her my letters. I should have known he hadn't told Toni the truth. The entire time I was in jail he never once visited or wrote me. I know technically he wasn't supposed to have any contact with me, but seriously, I was sitting in jail for a crime he committed. I gave up my life for him, and all I asked for in return was that he let my girl know the truth so she would wait for me. David had really let me down, but I never really got a chance to express any of this to him. I thought about how Jada has been towards me since I got out, and the fact that she doesn't know the truth still bothers me. My closest friends had turned against me, and all because I was trying to do the right thing by ensuring my best friend would be around to be a father for this child.

Vince and I met for breakfast and then headed to the courthouse for our meeting with the judge. Vince seemed very nervous and uptight during breakfast and on the cab ride over to the courthouse. I tried to make him more comfortable, but it didn't seem to help.

The meeting with the judge was very interesting. First, I was struck by how different he was than the judges I had encountered in criminal court. Even though this was an informal meeting in his chambers, I expected something much different. He was dressed in very casual attire—khaki pants, polo shirt, and sneakers. He also appeared to be very young. His demeanor was extremely pleasant, not accusatory and demeaning like what I had experienced previously. After introductions, Judge Johnson offered us a seat, and we got started.

"So, gentlemen, I would like for each of you to explain to me how you ended up in this situation."

I had already decided to be open about my jail time, so after taking a deep breath, I started with my story first.

"Well, Judge, before we get into that I need to explain a few things to you about my current situation. I do have a criminal record."

Judge Johnson raised his eyebrow. "Okay, Mr. Royal I need to know more information about that."

I moved forward in my chair, looked him in the eye, and started to explain.

"During my senior year in college, I was at a party, and of course, there was a lot of drinking going on. I will not go into the graphic details, but things got out of control, and unfortunately, a young lady got hurt. I served my time, which was seven years, and I have been out for a little over a year now. I am compliant with all of my post-release conditions."

Knowing the judge had probably heard his share of stories where the convict claims to be innocent, I purposely left out the part about me taking the blame for my friend. Judge Johnson took notes and nodded as I spoke. After a brief pause, I continued.

"Another area of concern may be that my job as a sports recruiter requires a lot of travel. I realize this will prove to be a challenge if I'm going to try to raise a child."

He nodded his head to acknowledge he heard me and then said, "Thanks so much for being up front and honest with me, Benjamin. We do our own background checks, but I'm impressed that you were forthright regarding your prior conviction." He then looked at Vince and then back at me before saying, "Next, I would like to know a little bit more about how you two know each other."

Vince was very nervous and had barely said anything since the introductions, so again I took the lead.

"Well, Your Honor, Vince and I really don't know each other besides recently when we decided to look for the child that was put up for adoption. We happened to have dated the same girl during college eight years ago."

"Oh, I see. Well, where is this young woman? Why isn't she here with you today?" he asked.

I looked to Vince before replying just to see if he was going to finally open his mouth and say anything. When it was clear he wasn't, I answered.

"Well, sir, Toni recently had a baby. She's married now and has moved on with her life. She's expressed that she is not interested in participating in this child's life since she is working on building a life with her husband and son."

I don't know why, but I felt the need to explain a little more to him about our past and how Toni ended up dating both of us around the same time.

"Sir, Toni and I dated all through high school and college. We had a fight and broke up for a few months. It was during this time that she started dating Vince briefly."

The judge looked to Vince to confirm that my story was accurate.

Vince cleared his throat and finally spoke. "Um, yes, Your Honor, that is correct. My relationship with Toni was very brief and casual. We met at a party and only went out a few times. We didn't attend the same college and eventually lost touch."

"Okay, I understand that. Now explain to me how you have all ended up back in each others' lives years later."

"Well, sir, Toni and I share several close friends, and they all live close to each other in Harrisburg, Pennsylvania. The strange coincidence is that Toni met and eventually married Vince's close friend Darien."

As I explained, I thought about how odd this must sound to someone who lives in a big city like Chicago, but Harrisburg was a small town even though it was the capital of Pennsylvania. Everyone knew everyone, and to have a close circle of acquaintances with such intertwined lives was commonplace in Harrisburg.

Judge Johnson stopped writing, put his pen down, and looked at Vince and then to me.

"Okay, wait. So let me get this straight. You're telling me that Toni, the woman who gave birth to Derrick, is now married to Mr. Smith's friend?"

Vince and I nodded our heads yes, while Judge Johnson started shaking his head. Then he picked up his pen and started writing again.

"Um um um. I've heard a lot of stories in my day, but this one is unbelievable. Well, I thank you both for answering my questions and explaining how we ended up here. Now let me tell you a little bit about Derrick and his situation."

Even though Vince had filled me in on what the attorney told him last night, I wanted to hear everything straight from the judge. Again, I raised myself up in my chair and gave Judge Johnson my full attention.

"Derrick is the child's name, and he's eight years old. Derrick's adoptive parents divorced two years ago and have been in the middle of a custody fight over him since that time. I have had the unfortunate privilege of working on this case the entire time." He paused to allow us time to absorb the information he had

24

given us and to see if we had any questions. Since neither Vince
nor I spoke, he continued.

"The custody battle has been rough on Derrick. As a result,
he's in counseling, which I have to tell you must continue even
after we establish paternity and I make my decision as to who will
end up having custody of this young man."

He stopped again and put his pen down on his desk. He
looked back and forth between the two of us, put his elbows on his
desk, leaned forward, and clasped his hands together.

"Next, I need each of you to tell me what your intentions
will be if a DNA test confirms you are the father of this child."

Since I had been doing most of the talking up to this point,
and since I was still a little unsure how I wanted to handle this if I
was in fact Derrick's father, I decided to let Vince answer the
judge first. After a brief silence, Vince started.

"Well, Your Honor, I have thought long and hard about
this. If the DNA test confirms that I am Derrick's biological father,
it is my intention to seek full custody of him."

Vince's voice cracked when he got to the words full
custody. I could tell he was very nervous.

"Mr. Smith, please tell me how you plan to manage an
eight-year-old like Derrick who is going to have scars from being
involved in this custody battle for the past two years, not to
mention the scars from being separated from the only parents he
has ever known."

Vince sat up in his chair and leaned in towards the judge.
His entire demeanor changed. It was as if he had suddenly been
energized and had a confidence about him that wasn't there just
two minutes ago.

After clearing his throat, Vince responded, "Your Honor,
based on what my attorney has shared with me about Derrick's
current situation and this nasty fight for custody by his adoptive
parents, I honestly feel I can provide a much more stable
environment for him. From everything I've heard, it seems like he
is already living in a volatile environment, and you already
mentioned he is currently in counseling. One of the issues right

now is the constant back and forth between his parents and their bickering. If he were with me, there would be more stability."

I was very impressed with how well Vince handled the judge's questions, and his answers really made sense. I thought he made good points, and it seemed the judge did, as well. He took a lot of notes and seemed to be nodding in agreement.

After finishing up his notes, Judge Johnson finally said, "Well, it's very clear to me that neither of you were given a fair chance to relinquish your parental rights. Therefore, I am going to issue the order for the paternity test. In fact, since you're both from out of town, I am going to arrange for the test to be done today."

Vince and I looked at each other and smiled. I was glad we were going to have a chance to get this part out of the way now without having to make a return trip.

After telling us that Derrick's adoptive parents would be notified to bring him in for testing, Judge Johnson gave us instructions on where to go to give our samples. We would have to wait a week for the results, though. He explained he would be delaying his decision on the custody of Derrick until the results came back from the paternity test. Once we got the results, our attorney could file whatever petitions on our behalf for custody, and then the judge would render his decision. The entire process could take about a month. I was relieved for the additional time to consider my options and decide what I wanted to do. However, Vince was less than thrilled about the wait.

Vince and I headed to the facility to have our DNA samples taken before going our separate ways to head home. I decided to have my results delivered to David, Sr.'s office. Unlike Vince, I had not hired an attorney to deal with any of this. David, Sr. had offered to assist in any way he could, so I was going to take him up on that offer.

Vince

After Benjamin and I gave our DNA for the paternity test, we shook hands and wished each other luck. We took separate cabs even though we were both headed to the airport. During the ride, I thought about the things I had told the judge. I was confident I could provide a stable home for Derrick if he were in fact my son.

I didn't mention any of this to my parents. Of course they knew about Gina and I not being together and why, but I couldn't bring myself to tell them about this situation. Although embarrassed about it, I knew I would have their support if Derrick were mine.

I continued to ponder what I would do if he were mine. I thought about all the things I did with my father when I was young. I knew Derrick had a rough few years with his adoptive parents. So, my goal would be to create some stability in his life. I knew it wasn't going to be easy, though. I also had to come to grips with what I would do if he were not mine. Part of me knew this search was to keep my mind off of the pain from Gina's betrayal, and if Derrick weren't mine, I would have to find something else to occupy my time.

Every time I thought about Gina, I felt heaviness in my chest. The day Samantha was born is a day I will never forget. To go from complete joy and happiness to utter sorrow, disappointment, and rage was a lot for anyone to take. Maybe I wasn't handling this well by not allowing myself to talk about it with anyone, but it was too painful. My father tried to talk to me a few times, but I wasn't really open to it. I felt like no one else in the entire world could understand the pain I felt. How could they? Thankfully, most people don't have to endure this type of betrayal and pain in their lives.

Every now and then, I allowed myself to think about whom Samantha's father could be. I forced myself to look for signs that Gina had been seeing someone else, but I couldn't remember anything that seemed out of the ordinary. My boy Darien was quick to point out the time Gina and I broke up right after Valentine's Day. We were apart for about six weeks or so. Based on when Samantha was born, the timing fit. One could argue that since she was with someone while we were apart, it shouldn't matter. Yet, it did matter because she was dishonest about it. Once she discovered she was pregnant, she should have been honest about the fact that the child may not have been mine, giving me a chance to decide how I wanted to handle the situation. Gina was selfish and wanted to control the situation as much as possible. For the life of me, I cannot figure out how she thought she could pass off a white baby as mine as dark as I am.

My thoughts were interrupted by the cab driver's abrupt stop at the terminal.

As the plane took off, I pushed the thoughts of Gina out of my mind and decided to focus on my music career and how to continue moving it forward. I would deal with Gina another day. I smiled as I thought about running into Greg, and how he had inspired me to think about opening a studio and teaching piano to kids. If Derrick were mine, he could be my first student.

Chapter 4

Jada

Lying in my bed, I thought about the past year. Today was the one-year anniversary of the accident that claimed my late husband David, Jr.'s life. When he first died, it felt like time stood still forever. Now, as I lie here, I am amazed at how quickly time seems to have passed me by. I thought about the holidays and how difficult they were without David. I wish I could explain to someone how hard it is to be alive when the only person you have ever loved and felt connected to is gone. I wondered if I would ever be able to love again. The love David and I shared was so pure and perfect; is it even possible to experience something like that twice in your lifetime? Most people aren't even blessed to find that type of love once.

I hugged the pillow tight against my chest and closed my eyes, trying to imagine David's face, his skin in the summertime when it was tanned, his baby blue eyes, and his crooked nose that never healed properly from an old high school basketball injury. Oh and that dimple on his left cheek. I sighed heavily as I remembered how cute he looked when he smiled and that dimple showed. I reminisced about how good he smelled and how his touch felt against my skin.

This had become my morning ritual. I needed to get up and get my day started, but I was stalling on purpose because I knew today would be a very difficult day. It was time to make some changes; it was time to move on.

Gina

I decided to get up early and head to the cemetery to visit David's grave. I knew Jada would be there today at some point, and I didn't want to risk running into her. As I approached the section where his grave was located, I noticed another car and a woman standing by his grave. Since I didn't recognize her, I became very curious about who she was and why she was there. So, I parked and hurried over towards the grave. As I got closer, I could hear the young woman speaking in a soft voice. Not wanting to startle her, I stopped and waited for her to finish speaking. When there was a break in the one-sided conversation, I interrupted.

"Excuse me. Who are you?"

Startled, the unidentified woman spun around and backed away from me. She looked very young…well, at least younger than me by a few years. Harrisburg was a pretty small city, so I was fairly certain she was not from around here. She stood about 5'10" and had a nice build, but not too skinny like a model. Her shoulder-length hair was blonde, and her skin was a bronze color, like she tanned often. What caught my attention the most were her piercing brown eyes. It seemed as if she was looking straight through me. I also sensed sadness and fear in them.

"Who are you?" I asked again. "Why are you visiting David's grave?"

She looked around like she was looking for an escape route and then replied, "Um, my name is Victoria. I…I am…I mean, I was a friend of David's from college."

I sensed her fear, so I relaxed a bit and moved towards her with my hand extended. "Hi, Victoria. My name is Gina, and David was a friend of mine, also. Nice to meet you."

"Nice to meet you, too," she responded.

I could tell she was still very nervous and uncomfortable, while I was still very curious.

So, I asked, "Where are you from? You're not local, are you?"

"No. Um, I'm from Ohio," she replied.

"Really? So you knew David from college? You look a lot younger than he was."

She shifted from one foot to the other and then started looking around again. Finally, she said, "Um, well, Gina, it was really nice meeting you, but I really have to get going."   As she turned to leave, I reached out and grabbed her arm. "Wait, Victoria. I would like to talk to you a little more about how you knew David."

She moved her arm to release my grip and asked, "Why do you care?"

"Well, I'm a reporter, and I did a story on David and his life before he died. I'm working on a follow-up story now, which is why I came here today. I was hoping to run into some of his friends and family so I could interview them."

She continued to look around as if she was expecting someone. Finally, she said,
"Look, I have to go, so I can't talk to you right now. Give me your business card, and I'll contact you later so you can interview me."

Not trusting that Victoria would call me, I reached into my purse and grabbed two cards. I handed one to her, and on the other, I asked her to write down her number so I could get in touch with her. She reluctantly gave me her number and turned to leave. As I watched her walk away, I reached for my cell phone and dialed the number she gave me. When it started to ring, I watched her reach into her pocket to retrieve her phone. Yes, she had given me the right number. I had to be sure before I let her out of my sight. Before she answered, I disconnected the call.

As I watched Victoria drive away, I noticed another car headed in my direction. I quickly realized it was Jada. With not enough time to get to my car without being seen, I headed over towards the mausoleums to hide until Jada left. I didn't want to run into her today, even though I often thought about what I would say if I ever did.

Today, as I stood in the shadows and waited for Jada to finish her visit, I thought about how much of a difference a year could make in one's life. A year ago, I was pregnant with Samantha and getting ready to marry Vince. I always wondered if I was the last person to talk to David before the accident. I remember the phone call when I broke things off with him because I was marrying Vince. Now, a year later, Vince and I are no longer together; our marriage didn't last long after the birth of Samantha.

Vince was a great person who loved me like no one had ever loved me. I had no idea why I had been unfaithful to him with David. We technically were not together when I started sleeping with David, but it didn't matter. In the end, Vince married me thinking I was pregnant with his child. Through the entire pregnancy, I suspected the baby might be David's, but I held out hope that Vince would be the father. I guess the honest thing would have been for me to be truthful with Vince, but I knew he would have never married me if he knew I had been with someone else.

People say childbirth is the most painful thing you will ever experience in your life. However, you forget the pain as soon as you hold your newborn baby. That was not the case for me. My labor lasted over thirty-six hours and was very painful. Unfortunately, I will never forget the experience because of the look on Vince's face as soon as they held Samantha up. Vince didn't even say a word; he just looked at me with tears in his eyes and walked out of the room. He didn't have to say anything. I knew as soon as I laid eyes on her that she was not his. Samantha belonged to my white lover, David. I cried while holding her in my arms because she was the most beautiful thing I had ever seen in my life. I also cried because I knew she would never know her father and the wonderful person he was.

My mother was in the room with me and beaming with joy. She was very pleased that Samantha didn't belong to Vince. My mother was the only person who I had confided in during my pregnancy that the baby might not be Vince's. She and my father never wanted me to marry him anyway. They were old fashioned and didn't approve of interracial couples. The thought of their first grandchild being of mixed descent must have kept them both up at night.

Now I found myself a single mother going through a nasty divorce and wondering how I got here. I didn't want a divorce. I really wanted to try to work things out with Vince. He was very bitter, though. He barely spoke to me and couldn't look at me. I tried many times to explain everything to him. I wanted him to know who the father was and that I didn't cheat on him when we were together. I also wanted him to know that David was dead, so there was no threat of him coming back into my life.

Vince just wanted me out of his life. I always felt others were influencing him, like his friend Darien, but I couldn't prove it. On the day Samantha was born, Darien was in the waiting room while I was in labor. I can only imagine what he said to Vince when he stormed out the way he did. Darien and I never got along, and I'm sure he took the opportunity to fill Vince's head with all kinds of negative things about me.

Darien and I knew each other from my "prior" life, which is how I liked to refer to it. Long before Vince and landing the job with the television station, I worked at the gentleman's club on Route 22. Being the player he is, Darien frequented the club on a regular basis. The only thing I liked about Darien is that he never divulged my secret to Vince. I know there was many times when he would have loved to let Vince in on my little secret, but even when I treated him like crap, he never did. However, that only made me more suspicious of him because I felt like he was holding it over my head and just waiting for the perfect time to drop the bomb. Darien once told me that the only reason why he didn't tell Vince was because Vince loved me so much and he didn't want to hurt him.

Jada

I stood by my husband's grave on the one-year anniversary of the accident that claimed his life, and I found myself wondering what had happened in the last year. It seemed like just yesterday my life was perfect. I had a wonderful, loving husband, two great kids, and a successful career as Director of Marketing at American Health Products. In an instant, my world changed forever.

The kids wanted to come and I would bring them later, but right now, I needed some time alone to talk to David. At first, I sat there quietly, silently meditating. As I had done so many days since the accident, I found myself asking God, *Why me? Why him?*

The kids missed him, but they seem to have bounced back and moved forward more easily than I have. In fact, I know I haven't moved on. It's a year later, and I'm still asking why. Today, I decided I would talk to David and ask him if it was okay for me to move on. Up until now, I felt like I would be betraying him if I started to live a normal life and didn't mourn him every day.

I closed my eyes and imagined David's face. I always tried to remember what he looked like the last time I saw him. I loved his smile and missed it. Once I had a good image, I started talking to him.

David, I know that somehow you can hear me. Baby, words cannot express how much I miss you. It's been a year, but the ache in my heart is as strong and vivid as it was the day you died and left me wondering how I could possibly live without you. You were and will always be the love of my life. No one will ever be able to take your place in my heart. The love we had is what most people dream about, but we lived it. I realize now that it is time for me to start living my life without you. I need to stop living in the past and look ahead to the future. I guess what I'm asking is for your blessing to start my life over again. It is something I never thought I could do, but I have reached a point where the loneliness is making each day more unbearable than the previous day. I continue to live my life as if you're going to walk through the door at any moment. I need to close this chapter of my life and start building a new life for our children and myself.

After I finished talking to David, I sat and remembered as many things about him and our times together as I could. It was a beautiful day; I looked around the cemetery to see how many other people were taking advantage of the weather to pay their respects to their lost loved ones. I didn't notice too many people, but I did see another car near where I parked. I scanned the area nearby but didn't see anyone.

I checked the time on my watch and decided to head back to the house. The kids would be awake soon, and I would bring them out so they could spend some time here, as well. As I walked away from his grave, this time felt a little different from all of the other times I had walked away over the last year. I felt a sense of peace or closure.

Gina

The sound of Jada's car starting interrupted my thoughts of the past. I waited until she was well out of sight before walking over to the gravesite. As I approached his tombstone, I felt a sense of sadness come over me. I was sad for Samantha, me, and even Jada and his other kids. David was such a great person. Even a year later it was hard to come to terms with this tragedy. I sat down and quietly meditated, then talked to David about Samantha.

Jada

As I was driving away, I had a strange feeling and decided to go back, wondering about the car I saw parked near mine. While coming back around, I saw her—the white women from the funeral, the reporter. She was walking towards David's grave. This time, I pulled my car slightly away from hers, then sat and watched her for a few minutes. After I saw her sit down and get comfortable, I decided to get out of the car and approach her. I had to know why she was visiting my husband's gravesite.

As I approached, she did not move. It seemed as if she was praying, so I decided to wait until she finished. Once she turned towards her car to leave, she would see me. Finally, she finished her prayer, or whatever, and got up to leave. As soon as she turned around, I started walking towards her.

"Excuse me, miss. What are you doing here?"

She obviously had been crying. She stopped dead in her tracks and stared at me. I recognized the sadness in her eyes, which looked like the same sadness mine had for the past year. The only difference is her eyes were blue. A lighter blue then David's, but as I looked into them, they reminded me of his.

"Excuse me," I repeated. "Why are you at my husband's grave?"

Still no response. She just reached into her purse to grab a tissue to wipe her eyes.

"Look" I said, "I just want to know who you are. I recognize you from my husband's funeral, but can you please just tell me your name?"

She hesitated and then took a step forward with her hand extended. "My name is Gina," she answered.

I extended my hand, as well, and as we shook.

"Hello, Gina. I'm Jada, but I'm guessing you already know that, right?"

She responded by nodding her head; she never took her eyes off mine.

"So, Gina, may I ask why you are here?"

"Listen, Jada, now is probably not a good time for us to talk. I know today must be a very difficult day for you."

"Yes, it is, but your presence here is making it even more difficult. So, can you just tell me why you're here?"

She seemed like she was thinking about what to say to me. After a minute or so, she finally said, "David and I were friends. I interviewed him a couple of years ago, and we kept in touch. I happened to be in the area, so I came by to visit."

Although I didn't buy her story, I decided to play along because I needed to get home to the kids and was not in the mood for any drama today.

"Okay, Gina, I guess that makes sense. I would hope if there was more to your story, you would be woman enough to tell me about it now to my face."

She nodded her head yes and said, "Jada, I would like to talk to you, but now isn't the time. Can I get in touch with you later? Maybe we can meet for lunch."

That sounded like a good idea because I had a feeling she and I needed more time than we had right now to discuss her connection to my husband. So, we exchanged numbers and parted ways. Both of us looked back over our shoulders at the other as we reached our cars. As I got into my car and drove off, I wondered what was really going on, and I knew I had to find out as soon as possible.

Chapter 5

Jada

I was still a bit shaken up about my encounter with Gina as I drove towards the house. So, I decided to call Toni to talk to her. She was still at home on maternity leave. When I called, she picked up right away, whispering. I assumed this meant Lil' Darien was sleeping. She confirmed it when she asked if she could call me back in a few minutes. I told her to call me right away because I needed to talk to her as soon as possible. In less than five minutes, my phone rang, and it was Toni.

"Hey girl," I answered. "How is my godson doing today?"

"He's good, girl. Just spoiled rotten of course. How are you doing? Did you go to the cemetery already today?"

"Yes, I did. That's actually why I was calling you. I ran into a woman there visiting David's grave."

"Really!" she screamed into the phone. "Who was she? Did you approach her?"

"Yes, I approached her, and her name is Gina. You know the reporter who did that interview on David a few years back?"

"Gina! Why in the world would she be there?"

"Wait a minute, Toni. You know Gina?"

"Yes, I do, and so do you. Gina was…well, she's still married to Darien's friend Vince."

"Oh yeah! She's the one who was getting married when Darien proposed to you."

"Yes, that's right. So what did you say to her? Why was she there?"

"She said she happened to be in the area and decided to stop by to visit his grave. She said they became friends after she did the story on him."

"Do you believe her?"

I thought for a minute and then responded, "Not completely. Yes, I know she interviewed him, but she was crying when I walked up. If they were just casual friends, why would she be at his gravesite crying?

"Hmm, I don't know, Jada. That sounds kinda fishy to me. So what did you say?"

"Well, she claimed not to have a lot of time, so we exchanged numbers and agreed to meet for lunch to talk further."

"Okay, so when are you going to call her to set that up? You want answers, right?"

"Yes, I want answers, but I'm going to wait a day or so before calling her. I need to focus on the kids and how they handle today first."

"That makes sense. Just let me know when you call her and when you plan to meet with her. If you need backup, I'll make sure I'm available."

This made me chuckle. Toni always tried to sound so hardcore, but she wasn't at all. She couldn't hurt a fly.

"Okay, Toni, I'll call for backup if I need it. Meanwhile, take care of my baby and let me know if you need anything for him, okay?"

Now it was her turn to laugh.

"Are you kidding, girl? This little boy has more stuff than most grown people I know. He's spoiled rotten. He doesn't need another thing."

I laughed with her. "Well, let me know when I can come over to visit. I haven't seen him in a few days."

"Okay, girl, I'll call you. I need to make sure my house is presentable first."

I ended the call just as I pulled up to my house and then sat in the car for a minute to collect my thoughts. Before running into Gina, I had a plan. I was going to start doing what I should have done months ago, clean my house. After David died, I threw myself into the kids, work, and helping Toni prepare for her wedding and the birth of the baby. Although I had gone through several of the stages of grief, denial, anger and depression, when I got to the acceptance step I got stuck. I couldn't bring myself to clean out his office. Toni and Darien had come over at some point and cleaned his clothes out of the closet for me. I simply couldn't bear the thought of removing any of his stuff from the house. His office was a different story, though. I wanted to handle that myself. Even David, Sr. had offered to help do it, but I refused.

In the beginning, David, Sr. came around often. He helped a lot with Tre and his therapy, but as time passed, his visits became less frequent. It was as if it was too painful for him to visit. I completely understood. I always liked David, Sr., but without David around things just weren't the same.

I made a mental note to check for any signs of Gina in David's office when I cleaned it out. I also considered checking with David, Sr. to see if he knew anything. He and David were much closer when it came to business affairs. Therefore, if Gina and David's relationship was purely based on business, David Sr. would know something about it. I knew he was coming up today to visit the gravesite, so I would ask him when I saw him later.

I went into the house and started getting the kids ready. Before we went to the cemetery, I wanted the three of us to sit down and talk. I tried to be open and honest with the kids about everything and allowed them to express themselves openly, as well. In the beginning, Tre seemed to blame himself for the accident. He felt if he had not gotten hurt, his dad would not have been in a hurry to get to the hospital. After some counseling sessions, he seems to have gotten over the guilt. They both bounced back much better than I had. I felt strange about today, almost as if I were forcing them to remember. Maybe it was best for them to move on. I decided to ask them if they wanted to go to the gravesite, and if they didn't, I wouldn't force them.

As we sat down at the table, I asked them if they wanted to go to the cemetery. First, I turned to Tre and was taken aback by how much he resembled his father. He had the same facial features, including that dimpled smile, but was just a darker complexion.

"Tre baby," I said, "if you don't want to go to the cemetery today, you don't have to go."

"Mom, I really want to go," he replied, looking like he was going to cry.

I reached for his hand and grabbed it. "Okay, baby. I just didn't want you to feel like I was forcing you to go."

"No, Mommy, I don't feel that way. I haven't been in awhile, so I want to go with you today."

I then turned to Jordan, who was a smaller version of me. Her eyes and facial features mirrored mine, but her eyes were light brown and her complexion was a golden brown color.

"Jordan baby, what do you want to do? Do you want to go to the cemetery with Tre and me today?"

Jordan didn't really like cemeteries, so I knew it was scary for her.

She hesitated before saying, "Mommy, I'm scared of that place, but if you hold my hand, I will go."

I smiled and reached for her hand. "I will hold your hand the entire time, Jordan." I then stood up and said, "Okay, guys, let's go ahead and head over now. Your grandfather is going to meet us there, and afterwards, we can grab some lunch. Okay?"

They both jumped up and headed towards the door. I thought about how proud David would be of them. They were both handling things so well.

Toni

As soon as I hung up the phone from talking to Jada, I called Darien at work.

When he answered, I immediately started talking. "Darien, guess what happened today?"

I heard him shifting the phone to his other ear and then he said, "What's going on, baby? I'm kind of in the middle of something right now."

"Well, we can talk more when you get home, but Jada just called and told me that she ran into Gina at the cemetery today. She was visiting David's grave, and when she walked up on her, she was crying."

"Hmmm, that does seem a bit strange," Darien responded. "But, baby, I'm really busy, so I can't talk now. I will try to come home a little early tonight so we can finish talking. Okay?"

"Okay, babe, no problem. I'm sorry to bother you at work. We'll talk later."

"Okay, and give my little man a kiss for me."

"I will. See you later, babe."

Things were starting to come together for me. Gina being at the gravesite was no coincidence. There had to be more to their relationship than meets the eye. I wondered if Jada was really going to pursue getting to the bottom of it or not.

Gina

As I drove away, I couldn't believe I had allowed myself to get caught visiting his grave by his wife. Thank goodness I didn't have Samantha with me. I think she looks just like David, and that would have been a dead giveaway. I considered if I should actually call to arrange a meeting with her or wait for her to reach out to me. Part of me felt relieved that we had bumped into each other. I wanted to get all of this off my chest and out in the open, but I could never figure out the best way to handle it.

For now, I would just wait for her to make the next move. If she contacted me, I would meet with her and tell her the truth about Samantha. I have nothing more to lose at this point. David is gone, and their marriage is over. I was actually more interested in contacting Victoria to find out more about her connection to David, Jr. I saw something in her eyes that looked very familiar to me, and I needed to get to the bottom of it.

I decided to call my mother to talk to her about the incident at the gravesite. I dialed my mom's number, and she answered on the second ring, sounding very excited to hear from me.

"Hey, Gina. How's my baby girl doing today?"

I rolled my eyes because I knew she always said that to annoy me. She was referring to Samantha, but baby girl is what my father used to call me when I was a little girl. My father and I used to be very close, but he has been so disappointed with some of my choices in my adult life that our relationship has been very strained.

"I'm doing fine, Mom," I finally responded, "and Samantha is good, too."

Mom chuckled on the other end of the phone because she knew she had succeeded in getting under my skin.

"Mom, I was calling to tell you about what happened today. I went to visit David's gravesite."

She interrupted. "Yes, I know today is the anniversary of his death, and I knew you were going to do that. So what happened?" The enthusiasm in her voice had clearly faded now.

"Well, I actually ended up running into his wife Jada," I answered.

"Really? So how did that go?"

"I think it went well, but she did seem a little curious and skeptical about my reason for being there. We exchanged numbers and agreed to meet for lunch to talk."

"Gina!" she screamed into the phone. "What on earth do you and that woman have to talk about?"

Before I had a chance to answer, she continued, "Gina, I told you once and I'm going to tell you again. Let sleeping dogs lies. I don't understand why you feel like any of this dirt needs to come up now. That man is long gone, and the only thing that will come out of the truth about him being Samantha's father will be heartache and pain for everyone involved. There is no benefit in it for Samantha, so why bother?"

I was crying now because I had heard it all before, and deep down, I knew she was right. Everything she said made sense. If there were some financial gain to be had, then maybe it would be worth pursuing, even with knowing Jada would be hurt in the process. That was not the case, though. David was just an athletic director, so there was no real financial gain.

"Yes, Mom, you're right," I finally responded through my tears. "I just panicked when I ran into her and didn't know what to say. I won't contact her, and if she reaches out to me, I'll stall or make excuses for not meeting with her."

"Good, Gina. That is really the best thing to do at this point."

However, while wiping the tears from my eyes, I decided if Jada contacted me, I would meet with her. The conversation would strictly be about business, though. I had interviewed David about his career, so I would leave it at that. We shared a common interest, sports. That was all Jada would get out of me.

"Thanks, Mom. I really appreciate you helping to bring me back to reality. I'm too emotional to go into work today, so I'm going to go home and work from there."

"Good. I think that's a great idea. So how is the new nanny that your dad hired for you working out?" she asked.

"Oh, she's great, and I love that I don't have to take Samantha out of the house every day. I really appreciate you and Dad paying for her for me."

"Gina, you know your father loves you. Even though he tries to act like he's mad at you, he still loves you and wants to do whatever he can to help you through all of this."

"Thanks again, Mom. I'm almost home, so I'm going to go now. I'll call to talk to you later."

I really was grateful to my parents for helping pay for the nanny. Since I had some flexibility with my job, it allowed me to work from home sometimes. Keeping Samantha at home with the nanny when I worked from home, I could see her in between naps, which made me happy.

As I pulled into my driveway, I immediately became sad again. The For Sale sign in the yard was a constant reminder that my life had taken a terrible turn for the worse the day Samantha was born. It's ironic how Vince and I had kept everything separate while we dated—separate apartments, separate bank accounts, etc.

As soon as we were married, we merged everything in an instant. We bought a house and started pooling our resources to prepare for our baby and our life together. Now we were in a legal battle of who had what first. The house had to be sold even though we were not going to make any money on it. Neither of us could afford it without the other. My parents offered to help me, but I honestly wasn't sure if I wanted to stay in the house that I had bought and decorated with Vince. I thought a fresh start might be better. However, the more time passed with Samantha and I in the house, the more I wanted to make this home. Maybe one day Vince and I would even reconcile once he knew the truth.

The mail carrier delivering mail interrupted my thoughts. I gathered my belongings and headed towards the front door. As I greeted the mail carrier, he handed me the stack of mail. Immediately, I noticed a letter from Vince's attorney, and I cringed. I entered the house and headed straight for my office. I needed to read this letter before I dealt with the nanny or the baby. I had a feeling it was going to be bad news. After opening the letter and starting to read it, I felt my blood pressure rising, and I shook my head in disbelief. Vince was requesting that I pay him back for all the money he spent on the wedding, including the engagement ring and the wedding bands. There was no way I would be able to come up with that kind of money on my own. He was bitter, and this madness had to stop. I hadn't attempted to make direct contact with him in over a month because our last conversation had been horrible. Vince was very hurt, and he took every opportunity to lash out at me, being verbally abusive whenever we spoke. I wasn't sure I was in the mood for one of his tirades today, but I needed to speak to him. So, I dialed his number. It rang four times before he finally answered.

"Gina, I have absolutely nothing to say to you. You need to have your attorney contact mine."

"Vince, please just hear me out for two minutes."

"I really don't have any patience for you or any of your games today."

"Vince, I just need a few minutes of your time. We're both adults. Can't we just talk like two adults for a few minutes?" The line was silent for a moment, and I thought he had hung up the phone. Then I heard a heavy sigh. "Vince?"

"Listen, I will give you exactly two minutes. Now what is it?"

"I just received a letter in the mail saying you want me to pay you back for the wedding and the rings."

"Yes, that's correct."

My eyes started to tear up. I knew he was hurt, but so was I. I loved Vince and I never wanted to hurt him like this.

"Vince, exactly how do you think I'm going to be able to do that?"

"That's not my problem, Gina. Is this why you were calling me?"

"Please, can we just sit down and talk about everything? This is ridiculous having everything going through attorneys. You and I used to be able to talk about anything."

"Gina, you betrayed me, cheated on me, and lied to me. How could you think you could have a white baby and pass it off as mine?"

This conversation was going nowhere. Therefore, I decided to end the call before things got worse than they already were.

"I know you're hurt, and I apologize. I never meant to hurt you. What happened between us affected me, also. I'm a single mother now trying to raise a baby on my own, and I simply cannot afford to pay you back all of this money right now."

"Gina, you will have to work all of that out with your attorney and mine. I have nothing more to say to you."

Vince hung up, and once again, I felt as if I had lost the love of my life. Each time we talked, I ended up experiencing the same hurt and rejection. I didn't know why I continued to try to get through to him. After all, this entire mess was my fault. I'm the one who decided to try to trap Vince in the first place, but it backfired on me. He pushed me to that point of trapping him because he wouldn't make a commitment to me. We dated for over three years with no mention of marriage. In fact, even after he discovered I was pregnant, it took him awhile to agree to marry me. None of this would have happened if he had just proposed to me on Valentine's Day, as I expected he would. I don't know why I was expecting it, but I was, and when it didn't happen, I completely lost it. We had a huge fight and broke up. David had been waiting in the wings, and the next thing I knew we were seeing each other on a regular basis. Vince and I were back together in less than two months, and when we got back together, I decided to take matters into my own hands. I stopped taking my pills to get pregnant. Little did I know I was already pregnant with David's child.

How I got here didn't matter. I had to find a way out. I was going to have to swallow my pride and ask my parents for help. After all, they didn't pay for the wedding because Vince refused to accept any money from them. He knew they were less than thrilled with him anyway. So rather than add insult to injury, he decided to use his savings to pay for everything. I was going to have to call my father and ask him to give me the money to pay Vince back.

I dialed my father's number, and he answered on the third ring.

"Daddy," I said through tears, "I really need your help."

I heard a heavy sigh on the other end of the phone, which made the tears flow even faster from my eyes. All I ever wanted was for my father to be proud of me. No matter what I did, it never seemed to be good enough.

"What is it this time, Gina?" my father responded, sounding completely annoyed by my call. I cringed as he emphasized the word '*this*'.

"Daddy, I need a loan from you to pay Vince back. He's being completely unreasonable about the house, and now he wants me to pay him back for the wedding and the rings. I don't want to have to move, but I cannot afford to buy him out. Can you please help me?" I pleaded with him.

There was a long period of silence on the other end of the phone, and then finally he said, "How much do you need?"

Smiling through tears, I replied, "Thank you so much, Daddy. I promise you I will pay you back."

"How much do you need?" he interrupted, asking again.

I couldn't respond right away because I really had no idea how much I needed. I shifted the phone to my other ear and responded, "I don't know the exact amount, but I will find out and let you know as soon as possible."

To this, he simply said, "Call me with the amount, and I will make sure my accountant gets a cashier's check ready for you." After a brief pause, he continued, "And, Gina, I'm only going to say this to you once. I am very disappointed in you, the choices you have made, and the fact that you have a child with no father. Your mother and I raised you better than that. I will help you get out of this situation, but no more. This is it. Do you understand me?"

The tears were flowing freely from my eyes again as I sobbed uncontrollably. I knew I had disappointed my parents, but to hear my father express his disappointment this way felt horrible.

"Yes, Daddy. I understand you completely," I simply said and ended the call.

Too emotional to call Vince back to ask about the price to buy him out of the house, I decided to wait until tomorrow to make that phone call. I sat back and thought about everything my father said. Shaking my head, I wondered how I ended up here. I had been in a loving relationship with Vince, but things just weren't moving along fast enough for me. My impatience always got me into trouble.

Chapter 6

Victoria

As I drove away from the cemetery, I thought about how I had run into Gina, and although that was bad, I was glad it wasn't Jada or worse yet David, Sr. I knew I wasn't supposed to have any contact with David, Jr.'s family or anyone else involved in the incident. When I heard about David's death, I started to regret agreeing to the money under the condition of having no further contact. David, Sr. has always checked on me to make sure I had whatever I needed.

At first, it seemed like the perfect set up. All of my medical bills were paid for, as was my education. The more time passed, the more I thought about an innocent man being in jail because I took hush money. It bothered me, and I felt I needed to do something to make amends. I had to think about how to do that. Maybe running into Gina was the best thing. I might be able to use her and her connections to make things right. I wanted to find a way to get in touch with Benjamin without David, Sr. finding out. The last thing I needed was for him to cut off my financial arrangement. Also, I knew how powerful David, Sr. was and how far reaching his contacts were. I have knowledge of him using them to handle clients or anyone else who has gotten in the way of what he wants to happen.

Benjamin

When I checked my voicemail and heard the message from David, Sr.'s assistant, I knew right away the results were in. I waited a few minutes before calling his office. The answer I had been waiting for was finally here. I called, and David, Sr. answered.

"Benjamin, I have the results of the paternity test," he said. "Do you want me to tell you over the phone or do you want to come into my office?"

I hesitated, took a deep breath, and replied, "Just tell me over the phone, please, sir, and get it over with."

He let out a heavy sigh and said, "Benjamin, I have great news for you..."

Jada

As I approached the section of the cemetery where David's gravesite was located, I saw David, Sr.'s car. He was always punctual. As soon as I stopped the car, Tre and Jordan jumped out and ran over to him. I watched as he picked them up and hugged them tight. I knew that today had to be absolutely hell for Sr., losing his only son in such a tragic way. They had always been so close, and it was hard for me to imagine how David, Sr. kept himself busy now that Jr. was gone.

My thoughts were interrupted by David, Sr. walking towards me and calling my name. I got out of the car and walked in his direction. When we met, he gave me a hug and a light kiss on the cheek. Then he pulled back a little while still holding my arms. I looked at him, his eyes, and his facial features. A chill ran down my spine. I felt as if David, Jr. was looking at me through his father's eyes.

"How are you holding up?" he asked.

"I'm doing okay," I responded. My voice was a little shaky, but I smiled to cover up my pain.

The four of us walked over to the grave and stood there in silence for a few minutes. Then David, Sr. started to talk to David. Jordan held onto my hand very tightly and moved closer to me. I knew she was very uncomfortable being in the cemetery, and to listen as David, Sr. talked to her father like he was actually here was very strange to her.

After leaving the cemetery, the kids wanted to go to Friendly's for lunch. Tre rode in the car with David, Sr., and Jordan rode with me. During the drive to Friendly's, I decided I would mention to David, Sr. while we ate about running into Gina at the gravesite earlier so I could get his take on the situation.

We arrived at the restaurant and met up at the front door. The hostess seated us immediately. After everyone had placed their orders, I looked at David, Sr. and started.

"David, I went to the cemetery earlier this morning to have some private time with David before bringing the kids over to meet you."

He looked at me over his glasses as he slowly sipped his tea, as if waiting for me to continue and get to the point. So, I did.

"While I was there, I ran into Gina, the reporter who interviewed David, Jr. before."

He sat his tea down on the table; I had his undivided attention at this point. "Really? Did you approach her? What was she doing there?"

"I did speak to her. She simply said they were friends, and since she happened to be in the area today, she decided to stop by."

He resumed sipping his tea, and finally responded in between sips, "Well, how about you let me handle her? I'm not sure what she's after, but I have never had a good feeling about her ever since she was snooping around at the funeral."

He seemed bothered by what I had shared with him about Gina, but I decided not to press the issue any further.

53

"Okay, well, I don't plan to contact her any further. I will let you handle her, as you suggested," I simply said.

David, Sr. smiled, and we left the conversation alone. During the rest of our meal, he talked with Tre and Jordan about school and what was going on in their lives. I was lost in my own thoughts. Part of me wanted to let him handle it, but something deep inside was telling me that I needed to call Gina. I made a mental note to start working on cleaning out David's office tonight and to look for any traces of Gina.

Toni

Dear Journal,

First of all, today is the anniversary of David, Jr.'s death. It's a bittersweet day for me. One year ago today, I reconnected with Benjamin after over seven years of feeling lost and abandoned. He reappeared out of nowhere just as the tragedy of David's accident and death was unfolding. In the end, his timing was perfect. I often think about Darien and if I could have really allowed myself to let go of the past and love him freely had Benjamin not showed up when he did.

Things are going well for Darien and I. We bought a house together in Susquehanna Township and are settling into married life while raising our son. I am still out on maternity leave, and we are struggling with the decision about me going back to work. Darien wants me at home, but I want to keep working. I worked hard to build my career, and I don't want to give it up. Thankfully, I have a little more time to think about this before I have to make a decision.

I've also been thinking about how special I always felt Jada and David, Jr.'s relationship was. Now while writing this, I wonder was it as special as I thought. I just got off the phone with Jada, and she told me that today at the cemetery she ran into Gina, the reporter who David, Jr. worked with a few years ago. The odd thing was that she was at his grave and appeared to be crying. Jada seems a little concerned, but not as alarmed as I am about it. It seems to me that there was much more to their relationship than

54

what Gina says. All of this coupled with the fact that I know Gina's baby is not Vince's since the baby is obviously white and not mixed. I now think Gina and David were having an affair, and her baby that she tried to pass off as being Vince's is David's. What I still can't imagine is David cheating on Jada. I always thought their relationship was rock solid. Jada thought and still thinks he was perfect. Even now, the thought of him being anything less than perfect has barely crossed her mind. Jada wouldn't even consider anything like this, especially since she doesn't know about Gina having a white baby.

All of this drama around Gina's baby and not knowing who the father is has made me think about my child that I gave up. For some reason, I thought having another baby would make the longing for my first child a lot less. I was wrong. In fact, every time I look at Lil' Darien I wonder about my first child. Now that I have Lil' Darien, I understand the bond between mother and child, and deep inside, I long for that child. I wonder what he or she looks like, and what type of life they've had. I try to put it all behind me, but as each day passes while caring for Lil' Darien, my feelings for the child I gave up grow stronger.

This weekend we're having a gathering at Jada's house to celebrate the life of David, Jr. I am somewhat excited about the possibility of seeing Benjamin. It's been months since I've heard anything from him. Last I heard, he was busy building his career and had decided not to pursue looking for the child I gave up. He said he might later once he got back on his feet. After the fiasco with Gina and her baby, Vince had contacted me to ask for Benjamin's contact information. Vince wanted to pursue finding the child so we could determine who the father was. Now I know Vince and Benjamin are working together to locate the child, and I have mixed emotions about it. No matter which one is the father, it's going to be difficult for me to handle. As much as I love Darien, if I'm being totally honest with myself, I'm not sure all of my feelings for Benjamin are resolved yet. I also think about how Darien might handle things if Vince and Benjamin found the baby and it was determined Vince was the father.

At Jada's request, I sent Benjamin an email a week ago to see if he planned to attend, but haven't heard back from him yet. That reminds me. I need to log in and check my emails for a response later. Well, my little man is awake now, so I have to cut this short. I will keep you posted on things with Gina and also the search for the child I gave up.

By the time Darien arrived hours later, I had concluded that David was the father of Gina's child, but that he didn't know before he died. Once Darien sat down at the dinner table, I started to explain.

"Jada told me that when she walked up on Gina, she had obviously been crying at David's gravesite."

In between bites of his food, Darien nodded to acknowledge that he was listening. When I paused, he took that as his cue to respond.

"That does sound a little suspicious, but seriously, Toni, how do you go from her being at the gravesite crying to him being the father of her child? Isn't that jumping to conclusions?"

I was starting to lose my patience with Darien. He was taking this entire situation a little too lightly for my liking.

"Darien, Jada was my friend, and I don't want her to get hurt."

"I understand that, but really, what difference does it make now if David, Jr. is the father of Gina's baby?"

"I can understand why you would feel that way. Vince is already hurt because he knows Samantha is not his child. So, this information really doesn't affect him at all."

I sensed Darien tense up every time I mentioned Vince's name. Although Darien said he was over the fact that Vince and I had been together eight years ago, clearly it still bothered him. Not in the mood to get into a discussion about that, I decided to leave it alone for now.

I took a deep breath and finally said, "You're right. It really doesn't matter at this point. It's up to Jada to decide if she wants to pursue getting any additional information from Gina. It's none of my concern."

Satisfied with my response, Darien smiled at me and continued eating his dinner. I knew he felt like he had successfully convinced me to let it go, but I planned on digging deeper to get to the truth.

While cleaning up the kitchen from dinner, I thought about approaching Gina to get the truth from her. I decided to contact her at work. That way, I could avoid going through Vince to get her number. I didn't want to do anything to give Darien a reason to suspect there was anything going on between Vince and I. Also, I thought some more about Darien's comment about what good the truth would do at this point. True, all it would do is hurt Jada, but I had to know, and Jada deserved to know the truth, too. Therefore, I decided I would go directly to Gina.

After Lil' Darien was asleep, Darien started working on his laptop. So, I logged in to check my emails. I used to be on top of my emails every day. However, now that the baby was here, days would go by without me getting a minute to check them. When I logged on, I was happy to see I had a response from Benjamin, although his message was very brief.

Toni,
I do plan to come up to visit David's grave this weekend, and I will stop over to Jada's to visit with everyone briefly.
Benjamin

I was very surprised he didn't mention anything about the search for the baby I gave up. To me, his note seemed very cold and distant, which was odd because I knew deep in my heart that Benjamin still had feelings for me. I thought about calling Jada to let her know he was coming, but after looking at the time, I thought it was too late. So, I decided to call her the next day to inform her.

As I continued going through my emails, I saw one from Vince. I looked over my shoulder to see where Darien was before clicking to open it. Since he was still busy doing his work, I went ahead and read it.

Toni,

I am writing to let you know that we have located the child you gave up. I would like to meet with you to discuss what I know and bring you up to date on what's next. Please email me back to let me know when would be a good time to meet.
Vince

I looked at the date stamp on the email and realized it was four days old. I wasn't sure what to do. I didn't want to mention anything to Darien right now, but I wanted to know what Vince had found out. I hated being sneaky; however, I knew Darien would get in one of his moods if I mentioned Vince's email. I decided to email Vince back and tell him to meet me the following day for lunch.

Vince,
Sorry I am just seeing your email. Can you meet me for lunch tomorrow? Email me back to confirm time and place, and I will be there. I want to know what you have found out thus far. I didn't mention your email to Darien because I would like to discuss this with you first.
Toni

The next morning, I got up early with Lil' Darien and prepared to run my errands. I had a very busy day ahead of me. After running downstairs to check my emails, I saw a response from Vince, who confirmed we could meet at noon at Applebee's by the Harrisburg Mall. I contacted Darien's mom to see if she would watch Lil' Darien for me while I ran some errands. She was more than thrilled to do so. I confirmed I would drop him off around ten o'clock. I wanted to have enough time to stop by the television station to speak to Gina. Darien was up and out of the house early, so I didn't have to worry about him asking where I was going today.

As I got Lil' Darien ready and all of his necessities packed up, I thought about my approach with Gina. Almost on cue, the phone rang; it was Jada.

"Hey, girlie, how are you this morning?" I answered.

"Girl, I'm glad I took off work today. I have so much to do to get ready for this little gathering you talked me into tomorrow night," Jada said.

Rolling my eyes, I responded, "Jada, you need to do something besides work and take care of the kids. Having this memorial for David and inviting your close friends over is a good thing."

Jada sighed heavily. "Yes, I guess you're right, but I have to make sure the house is clean and confirm everything with the caterers today. It's just going to be a very busy day for me, that's all. So what do you have planned today? Any chance you can bring my godson over here to see me?"

I thought for a minute. I didn't want to tell her about my plans to go see Gina, but I did want to mention the meeting with Vince to get her take on it.

"Jada, I'm not sure I will be able to do that today. I have a few errands to run myself. I'm actually headed out the door shortly."

Right on cue, she asked, "Oh, so where are you headed?"

"First, I'm dropping Lil' Darien off at his grandmother's house before going to pick up a few things from Target, and then I'm meeting Vince for lunch."

"Vince?" Jada screamed into the phone. "Why are you meeting with him?"

I switched the phone to my other ear. "He emailed me that he found the child I gave up and wants to talk to me about the next steps."

"Does Darien know about this?"

I hesitated for a minute, then responded, "No, Jada, he doesn't. I want to find out what Vince knows first before saying anything to Darien."

"Toni, you know that's not a good idea. Harrisburg is way too small to be meeting some man for lunch and think your husband won't find out about it. It's your business, but I think you need to tell Darien before you meet with Vince."

Jada was right. I don't know what I was thinking. The last thing I needed was for Darien to see me out having lunch with Vince. I had to call him before I met Vince.

"You're right. Let me go so I can call Darien now. Maybe I should invite him to meet with Vince and me so he hears everything at the same time I do."

"That sounds like a good idea, Toni," she responded. "Okay, I'll let you go, but if you get a chance later, bring my godson over to see me."

"Okay, I'll be in touch. Oh and, Jada, Benjamin responded to my email. He plans to come tomorrow, so please try to be on your best behavior. Okay?"

I heard Jada sigh heavily into the phone. "Okay, Toni. I will do my best."

After hanging up the phone, I immediately picked it back up and dialed Darien's number. He didn't answer, so I decided to leave him a message telling him about the meeting with Vince. I told him the time and the location, and invited him to join me if he could. At least this way he would know I tried to let him know before I met with Vince. Once I grabbed Lil' Darien and the rest of his things and, I headed out the door.

I loaded the baby into the car and headed towards Mama D's house. I decided to take Lingelstown Road down to Front Street. I loved to drive along the riverfront. It reminded me of my first real date with Darien. I smiled to myself as I remembered that night. Before I knew it, I was in front of Mama D's house, where she was standing in the doorway waiting for me to arrive. As soon as I opened my door and got out of the car, the door flew open and Joy came running out towards the car. I was surprised to see her.

"Joy, why aren't you in school today?"

Joy opened the car door and unlatched the car seat. I opened the opposite door to grab his diaper bag, while observing Joy handling the baby in the process.

Once she had the baby out of the car, she answered, "It's an in-service day." She then turned and headed towards the house.

I followed her and handed his bag to Mama D as I entered the house. I gave Mama D the rundown on his schedule, and she told me to take my time. She and Joy wanted to spend the day with Lil' Darien. At first, I had been a little concerned with leaving the baby with Mama D alone for an extended period of time, but with Joy there to help, I felt much better.

Chapter 7

Victoria

Several days have passed since I ran into Gina at the cemetery. I'd been thinking about calling her, but I wasn't really sure what I would say. I had mixed emotions about opening up this can of worms. I was torn between doing what is right and protecting my comfortable lifestyle that David, Sr. had been providing. I decided I was only complicating matters by thinking too much, and since Gina was a reporter, I should just let her ask me questions. So, I pulled out the business card she gave me and dialed her number. She answered on the third ring.

"Hello, this is Gina. How may I help you?"

"Um, hello, Gina. This is Victoria. We met at the cemetery the other day."

There was a brief pause, and then Gina said, "Oh! Hello, Victoria. How are you?"

"I'm fine." Nervous and wanting to get it over with, I got straight to the purpose of my call. "You asked me to get in touch with you to talk more about how I knew David."

"Yes, Victoria," Gina responded. "I would like to get more information about your relationship with David, Jr. When would be a good time for you?"

"I'm free now," I told her.

"Well, okay, I guess we can do this now. Can you hold on for one minute while I gather my notebook so I can take notes?" Gina said.

"Sure, no problem," I replied.

I heard some papers rustling in the background, and then she finally returned to the line.

"Okay, Victoria, why don't you start at the very beginning."

I took a deep breath and closed my eyes as I thought about where I wanted to start and if I would tell her the real story or the fabricated one that David, Sr. made up. I cleared my throat and started.

"I met David, Jr. at a college party. My friend Kelly and I were only sixteen, so we made plans to sneak into the party. Getting into the party was easier than we thought. Once we were in, we mingled and tried to pick up on who was who among the players. We were looking for basketball players because the team had just made it into the championships. We wanted to find the starters, the ones who had a sure shot at getting drafted into the NBA."

Interrupting me, Gina asked, "Why were you interested in the starters?"

"Kelly had this bright idea that if we could hook up with one of the starters and have sex with them, we could get money from them once they discovered our real age."

"Oh, I see. Okay, please continue," Gina said.

I could hear the disapproving tone in her voice, but I didn't care. I continued with my story anyway.

"Our plan was to stick together, but I spotted David and started following him around. Kelly was doing her own thing, and we eventually became separated. I thought I heard someone say several NBA teams were courting David, Jr., so he was my mark. I sparked up a conversation with him and began flirting. He was clearly drunk, and it wasn't long before he suggested we go somewhere to be alone. We ended up in an empty bedroom. One thing led to another, and we ended up having sex."

Gina interrupted again. "Which one of you initiated the

sex? At any point did he ask you how old you were?"

I had to think how to respond to Gina. Since some of this wasn't actually true, I wanted to make sure my answers made sense.

"No, he never asked my age, and once we got in the room, we did very little talking. The sex was definitely consensual, and when we were finished, as planned, I started to scream rape. After that, all I remember is seeing David turn towards me with fire in his eyes. He grabbed my shoulders, and my world went black."

"So you don't actually remember anything about the attack?" Gina asked.

"No. Almost a month later, I woke up in the hospital with my parents telling me that I was raped by a black man named Benjamin."

"So it is possible that Benjamin did rape you since you don't remember the attack?"

"Gina, I was confused when I finally woke up in the hospital, and yes, the last thing I remember was David, Jr. grabbing my arms, but that's it. Benjamin was nowhere around, so I know in my heart he didn't have anything to do with it. At first, I thought the same thing. However, when my parents kept telling me not to speak to anyone else except the lawyer who would be coming to get my side of the story, I became a little suspicious. When I finally spoke to the lawyer, who happened to be David, Sr., I wasn't asked for my side of the story. I was *told* my side of the story. That's when I knew something wasn't right."

"So David, Sr. visited you in the hospital to interview you about what happened? You never spoke to a police officer?"

"Yes, eventually I spoke to the police, but not until after David, Sr. told me what to say to them. In the end, I was advised to take a cash settlement and to never speak to anyone involved in the case again."

At certain points while telling Gina all of this, I felt like I could hear her jaw hitting the floor. When I finished, there was a period of silence on the other end of the phone.

Finally, Gina said, "Victoria, I want to do a feature story on you. I need to talk to my editor to get her approval, but before I do that I need to know if you're willing to go public with your story?"

I thought about how guilty I felt during the past few years for being a part of the lies that David, Sr. created. I also thought about my financial arrangement with David, Sr. and knew that taking this story public would put an end to that. However, I also knew this little scandal was only the tip of the iceberg. I knew this was not the first time David, Sr. was involved in something like this, so I made my decision.

"Gina, I want to clear my conscious finally. So, yes, I will agree to go public with my story."

"That is wonderful news, Victoria. I will check with my editor and get back in touch with you to discuss the next steps," Gina said, then we ended the call.

Gina

I sat in my office going over the notes from my phone interview with Victoria. I was intrigued and wanted to investigate everything further. Victoria's story about David, Jr. beating her just didn't sit well with me. She did admit not being able to recall anything after he grabbed her. So, there had to be someone else in the room that night. I knew David, Jr. and couldn't imagine him doing something so violent. The more I thought about it, the more excited I was to present my story idea to my editor, Susan. I needed something to sink my teeth into to keep me busy and get my mind off my impending divorce. I knew Susan would be all over this scandalous local story.

Just as I was putting the finishing touches on my email to Susan, my phone rang. I quickly answered, and the receptionist told me that I had a visitor. Since I wasn't expecting anyone, I was curious as to who it could be. Quickly, I got up and went to the lobby to meet my mystery guest.

When I entered the lobby, I recognized Toni right away. I had no idea why she would be coming to see me, but I walked over to greet her.

As I approached, she stood up and said, "Hi, Gina. Nice to see you today."

"Good to see you, as well, Toni," I responded. "How can I help you?"

Toni looked around and then lowered her voice. "Is there somewhere more private we can go to talk for a few minutes?"

"Yes, sure. We can go to my office." I motioned towards the hallway, and she followed.

As we walked towards my office, I realized this impromptu visit from Toni was probably the result of me running into Jada at the cemetery the other day. Once we were in my office, Toni and I both sat down. There was a brief period of silence before Toni spoke.

"So, Gina, why don't you tell me why you were visiting David's grave the other day?"

I stood up and started pacing back and forth before responding. I had to quickly think about how to play this one out with Toni. My mind was still reeling from the unbelievable story that Victoria had just shared with me. I knew Toni was a part of that, as well. I needed to try to find a way to make her my ally and not my enemy. Finally, I stopped pacing and sat back down.

While looking her directly in the eye, I said, "Obviously you think you know something. So, why don't you tell me what you think you know."

Now it was Toni's turn to stand up.

"Simply put, Gina, I believe there's much more to your relationship with David, Jr. than you let on. Ever since Jada told me about running into you, I've been thinking about all the reasons why you would be there. I can only come up with one conclusion. I believe you and David were having an affair, and that your baby is David's. We both know it doesn't belong to Vince."

After she finished, she took her seat again, and we both just sat there for a few minutes looking at each other. I had to decide quickly if I wanted to come clean with Toni or not.

Without admitting anything, I decided to ask, "What difference does any of this make now? I mean, David is dead, and the paternity of my child has no direct impact on your life."

Toni smiled and responded, "Gina, it impacts me because Jada is my friend, and she has no idea at all that her husband had been unfaithful to her, let alone fathered another child. My interest in this is for my friend and her emotional well being."

Deciding to play on her loyalty to her friend Jada, I responded, "So if I admit to the affair and the possibility of my daughter being David, Jr.'s child, what will you do with that information? How is revealing this to Jada going to help her emotional well being?"

Toni thought for a minute and then threw a question back at me. "What do you want from Jada? Do you want her to know about you and David?"

I already knew the answer and didn't hesitate for a moment before responding.

"No. There's no point in her knowing the truth. It will only cause her more hurt, and it's unnecessary."

She smiled. "Good, then you and I are on the same page. The last thing I want is for Jada to find out about this and endure any more pain. So, I say we keep this between the two of us," Toni said as she started to gather her things and stood up to leave.

I thought about the information I had received from Victoria; I wanted to get Toni in on getting the truth out. I knew she wouldn't agree to it easily, so I had to think about how to approach her regarding it.

Since she seemed to be in a bit of a hurry, I said, "Toni, I'm still working on finishing up my follow-up story on David, Jr.'s life. Why don't you and I get together for lunch in a few days so I can get some additional information from you to finish my story on him."

She looked at her watch and then moved closer to the door. "Sure. Give me a call, and we can set something up." She reached into her purse and handed me one of her business cards.

I walked her back out to the lobby, where I stood and watched as she hurried to her car.

Toni

As I drove to meet Vince, I tried Darien again at the office, but my call went straight to voicemail. I was anxious to meet with Vince to find out what he knew about the baby I gave up.

Thinking about the conversation with Gina still had me shaking my head. I couldn't believe David had an affair and fathered another child. I was relieved that Gina had no intentions of telling Jada about any of it. After my talk with Darien last night, I realized he was right. David was gone, so there really was nothing good that could come from Jada knowing about his affair. I did wonder if there had been other women based on the number of single women who showed up at his funeral.

As I pulled into the parking lot of Applebee's, I spotted Vince's car. I scanned the parking lot to see if I saw Darien's car, but I didn't. I assumed he was tied up in meetings and wouldn't be able to join us. All of a sudden, I felt very nervous as I walked into the restaurant. He must have seen me parking, because he met me at the hostess station to direct me to our table.

"Hi, Toni. It's nice to see you," he said.

"Good to see you, too, Vince. Before you get started, I want to let you know I left Darien a message that we would be meeting here today in case he's able to get away and join us. I would like for him to also hear whatever it is you have to say."

Before responding, Vince shifted in his seat and looked around the restaurant as if looking for Darien. He finally said, "Okay, well, he's not here. So should I wait or do you want me to get started?"

Now it was my turn to look around; I also checked my cell phone. No missed calls or messages.

So, I looked at Vince and said, "Well, I guess he's not coming. So, go ahead and tell me what you've found out thus far."

"Toni, before I begin, I need to know how much you want to know. I also need to know if you plan to change your mind about not having any dealings with the child."

69

My heart started to race as I took his statement to mean he had located my baby. Nervous, I took a sip of my water.

"So you have located the baby...I mean, the child?"

Vince nodded his head yes.

"Okay, so tell me where he or she is. What's going on?"

Vince put his hand up to stop me.

"Toni, before I answer any of your questions, you have to answer mine. I need to know where you stand before I give you any information."

I already knew the answer, but couldn't figure out why it was so hard for me to say it out loud. In addition to wanting to know everything, I would want to meet my child as soon as possible.

Clearing my throat, I replied, "I have changed my mind. I've decided that if you find my baby, I would like to meet him or her."

Vince interrupted me. "Him. It's a boy, Toni, and his name is Derrick."

Immediately, my eyes filled with tears, and I reached inside my purse for a tissue.

"So tell me what you know about him."

Vince shook his head. "It's not good, Toni. Are you sure you're up for this?"

I immediately switched into protective mother mode.

"What's wrong with my baby, Vince? Please tell me everything."

Just then, I felt a hand on my back, and I turned to see Darien standing behind me. Vince got up and gave Darien a hug, then sat back down. Darien looked concerned because I was obviously upset. He looked from me to Vince and back to me again. Vince sensed his concern and started to explain.

"Darien, I was just starting to tell Toni what I found out, but I was warning her that it's not all good and she became upset."

Darien put his arm around me, then looked at Vince and said, "Okay, man, so spill it. What have you found out?"

"It's a boy, and his name is Derrick," I blurted out.

Vince continued and said

"Yes, I found the child Toni gave up," Vince stated. "And it's a boy."

"So what else do you know?" Darien asked.

"Derrick's adoptive parents divorced two years ago, and they are currently in the middle of a nasty custody battle right now. Benjamin and I went to—"

Darien interrupted Vince. "Wait. Benjamin is involved in this, too?"

"Yes," Vince responded. "After we located Derrick and found out about the custody battle, my attorney petitioned the court to ask that they perform a paternity test on me and Benjamin so we can determine who is the father. That way, we can petition the court for custody before the judge renders his final decision on the pending custody case."

At the mention of Benjamin's name, my entire body tensed up. Darien sensed it and grabbed me closer, while Vince continued to explain.

"Benjamin and I went to Chicago a couple of weeks ago to get tested and meet with the judge who is presiding over the custody case. We were both tested, and the results just came back yesterday."

Darien and I looked at each other, and then he asked, "So which one of you is the father?"

It was as if everything started to move in slow motion. The sound was muffled, and the room started to spin. I felt as if I was going to be sick to my stomach.

I closed my eyes, and all of a sudden, I was back in Chicago all alone, pregnant, and trying desperately to get in contact with Benjamin. I couldn't understand why he would shut me out and simply abandon me just because of a career-ending injury. It just didn't make sense. Benjamin and I were so close; we were soul mates. I could not imagine anything that would keep him from me.

I remembered the pain I felt before giving birth, when I made the decision to give my child up for adoption. I also remembered the pain of childbirth. I thought about how different the feeling is when you actually get to hold your child afterwards. I felt so cold and alone after giving birth all those years ago. When Lil' Darien was born a few months ago, I remember feeling so much warmth and love.

I could hear Darien and Vince calling my name in the distance. I felt Darien's arm around me. When I opened my eyes, the room was still spinning, and the nausea feeling got stronger. As I stood to head to the restroom, everything went black.

Chapter 8

Jada

After the kids were in bed, I went downstairs. I was expecting company tomorrow and wanted to make sure everything was in order. I can't believe I allowed Toni to talk me into having close friends over for a memorial. I knew I wouldn't have the energy to cook, so I hired a caterer and even had the cleaning service that David, Sr. hired for me do a little extra this week. Once I felt everything was in order for me to entertain, I decided to start going through the things in David's office. I could actually use the space for my own home office, but needed to clean it out first. While doing so, I would search for any mention of Gina in his planner or other notes.

I searched the room for the box of his personal effects from his office at the school. Upon locating it, I found his planner inside, and as I flipped through the pages, I noticed Gina's name a few times in the months leading up to the accident. I also noticed several other women's names and numbers; however there seemed to be a pattern with Gina. Her name appeared on the same days of the week and at the same times. The meetings with the other women did not appear to reoccur like the ones with Gina.

Suddenly, I felt foolish. I was allowing Toni's comments and drama to get into my mind and play tricks on me. My imagination was running wild; there was no way David had been unfaithful. There had to be a good explanation for those meetings. He was the athletic director, and he did interact with a lot of children. Therefore, he would have contact with their mothers, also. Still, the only one that seemed odd was Gina. Her name showed up repeatedly in his planner, and there was a pattern. I was definitely going to follow up with her to get more details.

While sitting at his desk, I looked around the office. He had at least a hundred books on the shelves. I remember when we were looking at this house. We both fell in love with the built-in bookshelves. There were lots of pictures of the kids and of the teams he helped coach over the years. I got up and walked over to the bookshelf to take a closer look. The memories these pictures evoked were bittersweet. David loved his job and working with the kids.

Wiping a tear from my cheek, I went over to the closet to see what was inside. There were a number of boxes, most of which were labeled. I decided I really didn't have the energy for this tonight, but just as I was closing the closet door, my eye caught sight of a labeled box wedged in between two other boxes up on the shelf. There was an envelope sticking out of it, so I decided to investigate further. I grabbed the box and pulled it down. The return address on the envelope was from a prison. I was all too familiar with prison mail because of all the low-life men my aunt associated with while I was growing up. It seemed like one of her "friends" was always locked up for one thing or another.

My attention shifted back to the envelope in my hand. It was addressed to David, and I couldn't imagine who would be writing him from prison. When I opened the envelope, there was another envelope inside that was addressed to Toni. I put the letter down and opened the box to find hundreds of letters all addressed the same way. The outside envelope was addressed to David, Jr., but inside, there was another envelope addressed to Toni.

I decided to take the box upstairs so I could inspect its contents. On the way, I grabbed a glass of wine. Once in my room, I took a stack of envelopes out and examined them further. They appeared to be in order by date. So, I searched for the envelope with the earliest date. While doing so, I thought about Toni. I wondered if I should call her to let her know about my discovery. Not all of them were opened, but the ones with the earlier dates were. I picked up the first letter and looked inside the envelope. There was a piece of paper inside that was addressed to David. I decided it was within my rights as his wife to read any correspondence addressed to him. So, I did.

Dear David,

Please pass the enclosed letter on to Toni. I miss her so much, man. I have to let her know where I am and what's going on. I cannot leave her in the dark. I thought I could do it, but the more time passes, the more I realize how hurt she will be. I explained everything to her in the enclosed letter and begged her not to tell Jada. I know Toni, and she would never do anything to hurt or upset Jada. I am certain she will keep this secret. I'm going to continue writing to her through you. Please pass these on to her so she knows I'm still thinking about her. I do hope my appeal works, because I cannot imagine staying in here for seven years.

There was more, but I stopped reading. My eyes kept going back to the sentence that read, *not to tell Jada.* I couldn't imagine what secret they were trying to keep from me. Now I had to know what was in the letter Benjamin had written to Toni. At first, I thought I should call Toni and tell her about the letters, but the more I thought about them keeping something from me, the more I talked myself into just opening the letter Benjamin wrote to Toni. I reached for my glass of wine and took a long sip before opening the letter addressed to Toni in the first envelope.

My dearest Toni,

There is so much I want to tell you, and I will write you every day and try to fill in as much of the details as possible. First of all, I love you and would never abandon you. I know by now you must think I have; however, I need you to know that is not the case. The truth is I'm in jail, BUT I need you to know I did not do what I have been accused of. I am in here now because I was trying to save my friend David Jr. from ruining his life.

David and I went to a party to celebrate with the team. There was a lot of alcohol, and David got really drunk. He ended up with some young girl in one of the bedrooms. They had sex. (David says it was consensual, but the girl cried rape.) David, in his drunken state, started beating the girl when she said he raped her. It was very bad, Toni. The young girl was in a coma. Thank God she survived, or I might never get out of here. I couldn't bear the thought of David ruining his life, and with Jada being pregnant, I knew she needed him. I know how important it is for a child to have their father around. I thought David, Sr. would be able to get a better deal for me. I never expected to be in jail and especially not for a minimum of seven years, which is what they are now saying. I am currently working with David, Sr. on my appeal, but if I don't win, I need to be prepared to be in here for the full seven years.

Toni, it's very important that you don't reveal any of this to Jada. She doesn't need to know about this unfortunate incident. It could ruin their lives, and they have a child together now. I will continue to write you to keep you up to date regarding what's going on with my case. I love you, and please, baby, wait for me. I know I'm asking a lot, but remember all the plans we had together? We can still do them, just a little later than we planned. Miss you like crazy.

Love Always,

Benjamin

After reading the first letter about twenty times, I opened them all, and throughout the course of the night, I drank wine and read every letter Benjamin had written Toni. I experienced every emotion imaginable: anger, disappointment, disgust, pain, pity, and jealousy just to name a few. In the end, I was very angry, and as the sun rose, I knew this little gathering tonight was going to be like nothing Toni, Benjamin, or David, Sr. would expect. I needed a couple of hours of sleep. Then I would get started on making a few changes to the plans for tonight.

Toni

Journal Entry

   Tonight is the night of the memorial gathering at Jada's house for David, Jr. I'm looking forward to the distraction, as I know Darien and I need something to take our minds off of the bombshell from yesterday afternoon. Even though Vince and Darien had been such close friends, when the three of us get together, it's always very awkward.

   Vince announced to us that he and I had a son together. I became so overwhelmed with emotion that I fainted right there in the restaurant. When I came to, Darien was carrying me out to the car. I think I took the news so hard because the child I had given up all those years ago was in pain, and immediately, I felt the pain. Darien initially took the news much better than I had thought he would. It wasn't until as we were getting in the car that Vince announced he would be seeking full custody that I sensed Darien getting uncomfortable. Before we parted ways with Vince, Darien just asked that he keep us up to date on the custody battle. The hardest question for me to answer was when Darien asked if I wanted to see Derrick. I looked at Darien with tears in my eyes and said, "Yes. I never thought I would want to, but now I do."

   When we got home, Darien held me close as I cried and told him over and over again how sorry I was about all of this. I wanted to talk to Jada, but I knew she had a lot on her mind right now. I felt like Darien and I had some tough times ahead of us. So, I suggested we go to counseling, but he refused adamantly.

   My journal entry was interrupted by Darien asking, "What time are we going to Jada's tonight?"

I knew Jada initially hadn't wanted to do anything special, but I thought it would be good to get everyone together to talk and share our feelings. I really did it as a way to get Jada to focus on something other than work or the kids. She really needed to start living again. I felt like she was still mourning David every day. She hadn't even cleaned out his office yet. It looked just like it did the day he died. After several months, I had finally convinced her to let me and Darien clean his clothes out of their bedroom. That was very painful for her, but we finally got it done.

Lil' Darien was going to his grandmother's tonight while Darien and I went over to Jada's house. Darien has been very supportive throughout everything we've been through this past year. He barely knew Jada when David died, but he embraced her as his friend, and we have been doing as much as we can as a couple to help her through this. Darien has even spent time with Tre playing ball with him or taking him out for ice cream as a way to bond with him.

"I'm going to check to see if she wants us to come early or not," I finally responded to Darien's question.

I decided to call Jada to see if she needed me to help her get things ready. I dialed her number and it rang several times, but she never answered. So, I left her a message to call me if she needed me to come over early to help.

I walked into the living room to tell Darien what time we were going, and I stopped in the doorway. Darien was lying on the couch with Lil' Darien on his chest. They both appeared to be sleeping. It was moments like this that I loved. A little over a year ago, I was asking myself if I would ever find love again after losing Benjamin. Now I have a wonderful husband and a newborn son. I also have another son who I gave up, but is now coming back into my life. All the love I have given out over the years to people who didn't deserve it is coming back to me twofold. God is good.

I thought about how Jada and David had always attended church with their kids every Sunday like clockwork. That is something I wanted to do with Darien and Jr. Growing up in church was not a big part of my life, but I believed in God and wanted to make sure Lil' Darien had a solid spiritual foundation to start with. Once he was old enough, he could decide for himself, but for now, I wanted church to be a part of his life. I decided to discuss it with Mama D later today when we dropped the baby off. I knew she attended church regularly and thought it might be good if we all went as family to the same church. She attended Imani African Christian Church, and from what I heard, the pastor there was dynamic. I also knew they had a nice nursery, and I heard the choir was out of sight. It was official. Attending Imani with Mama D was on my to-do list, and sooner rather than later.

I walked over toward the couch, sat down next to Darien, and gently touched his shoulder. When he turned towards me, I leaned over to kiss his lips.

I then kissed Lil' Darien, picked him as he slept, and whispered to Darien, "I'm going to take him upstairs so he can finish his nap in his crib."

He nodded while readjusting himself to get comfortable on the couch.

I smiled and said, "Oh and, Darien, I called Jada but she didn't answer. So, let's just plan on arriving around six o'clock, okay?"

He didn't respond, but I knew he heard me. I hugged Lil' Darien close to my body and slowly walked upstairs.

Chapter 9

Benjamin

After getting the news that I was not the father of Toni's baby, I sunk into a bit of a funk. Deep down, I had hoped I would be the father and that somehow having a child together would reunite Toni and me. If not as a couple, we could be closer friends as we worked together to raise our child. All of those dreams were out of the window now. I wasn't looking forward to seeing Toni tonight, but I told her I was coming. Besides, I wanted to see Jada and the kids. Even though Jada had developed this hatred for me because of what she thought I had done, I still cared for her deeply. She was part of the reason I made the decision to take the blame for David's crime.

As I drove north on Interstate 83 towards Harrisburg, I thought back to some of the happy times the four of us shared. We were thick as thieves back in our high school and college days. David and I grew up together since elementary school. We met the girls, Jada and Toni, in high school. David started dating Jada first, and since Toni and Jada were so close, we naturally ended up spending a lot of time together. Toni and I didn't start officially dating until the spring of our first year in high school. We were both seeing other people when we were first introduced, but because of the love affair of our best friends, we spent so much time together that we eventually grew apart from our other partners. We made it official during the spring dance. I remember us going skating every Sunday at the Seabrook skating rink, hanging out at Greenbelt Park, and going to the movies. How different things were now.

I wondered if this would be my last trip to Harrisburg. With David gone and knowing Toni and I were not going to reconcile, what would be the point of me coming back here again?

I switched gears and thought about what I would say tonight when it was my turn for my reflection. When I received the initial email invitation, it stated that everyone needed to be prepared to share a reflection about David, Jr. I decided to talk about our basketball years together. Those were some of the happiest times of my life.

I remembered how David and I became such good friends. In elementary school, he approached me during recess one day and asked me to help him with his free throw shot. He watched me play basketball and said I was really good. He wanted me to help him improve his game. I had natural talent, but I also spent hours at the recreation center in Springhill Lake practicing. Soon, David and I were spending all of our free time together either at the recreation center or at his house playing basketball. His game improved, and in junior high, he made the team. Even though he was not a starter, he was very excited. As I drove, I thought about some stories I could tell from high school that both Jada and Toni would remember, as well.

Vince

After breaking the news to Toni and Darien yesterday, I felt so alone. I didn't have anyone else to talk to about any of this. It was times like this that I missed Gina. Even though I was mad as hell at her, I still loved her. She was the woman I thought I would spend the rest of my life with.

Since I now knew I had a child, I decided I would break the news to my parents this weekend during Sunday dinner. My parents would be in total shock, but I hoped I would have their support as I embarked on this venture of fighting for custody of my son whom I have never met.

Before meeting with Toni and Darien yesterday, I met with my attorney to discuss the next steps. There was going to be a hearing next month where I would get to present my case for custody. My attorney felt I had a good shot at partial if not full custody. I had to come up with a plan to prove to the court how I would manage taking care of Derrick. One suggestion was that I move to Chicago as a way to keep him in familiar surroundings. If I did that, I wouldn't have any support around me unless I asked my parents to move, also. I had a few weeks to pull my plan together, and a part of that plan would include reaching out to Greg to see if his music business connection had come through or not. I could really use a break right now myself. I felt a little funny trying to ride on his coattail, but I have a son now who I need to provide for. I could hear my mother's voice telling me to pray about it, and that's exactly what I planned to do.

I also wanted and needed to sit down with Darien. I could sense the tension between us building ever since this all came out. Now that we knew for sure, we had to deal with our feelings open and honestly. I tried to put myself in his shoes to think about how I would feel. I surmised that his issue was he thought Toni and I might want to reconcile. I needed to reassure him that there is nothing between us at all and that he had absolutely nothing to worry about. I decided I would call to ask him to meet me for lunch to discuss things further.

Gina

As I walked around my house picking up toys, I thought about Vince. Thanks to my father, I was going to be able to buy him out so I could keep the house. I really missed him, but I had to face the fact that we would never reconcile. I had hurt him too deeply.

I was getting Samantha packed for her visit to my parents' house for the day. I loved her, but I also loved my alone time on the weekends. My mom loved having her only grandchild over, so it was our routine. On Saturdays, I would drop Samantha off and then go shopping or to the gym. Some days, like today, I would simply go home and work. I was working on putting the finishing touches on the story about David, Jr. and Victoria.

Just as I was about to walk out the door, my cell phone rang. I grabbed it and looked at the number. I didn't recognize it, but I always received calls from random numbers, so I answered it.

"Hello."

"Hi, is this Gina?"

I switched the phone to my other ear and said, "This is Gina. How may I help you?"

"Hi, Gina. This is Jada, David Wright's wife."

Completely taken by surprise by her call, I walked back into the house and put Samantha down.

"Yes, Jada, how can I help you?" I asked, trying to sound professional although I had no idea why I took that approach.

"I was calling to invite you to a memorial service we're having at my house tonight for David, Jr."

"Wow, tonight?"

"Yes," Jada responded. "I'm sorry for the short notice, but I just thought about it late last night that you mentioned you've been trying to finish your follow-up story on David's life. All of his close friends and family will be here tonight."

I thought for a minute before replying, "I'll have to change some things around, but I can make it tonight. What time should I arrive?"

Jada confirmed the time and the fact that Benjamin would be there, also. *Wow*, I thought after ending the call. *Things are really looking up for me.* I had the inside scoop on what happened between David and the young girl, and now I was going to get the opportunity to get Benjamin's side of the story.

I went back into Samantha's room to put some extra clothes in her bag. I would tell my mother that she needed to spend the night tonight because I had plans.

As I drove towards Hershey on Route 322 to my parents' house, I thought about the gathering and how to get the information I needed from everyone there. Based on Victoria's story, it was clear to me that Jada didn't know anything about David's involvement with her. I wanted to get Benjamin's side of the story, but I realized I wouldn't be able to broach that subject with him tonight, at least not directly. I planned to press him for information about his whereabouts for the past few years to see if I could get him to talk about his prison time. I hoped that I could get him to meet with me one on one to discuss the incident. The only person I wasn't looking forward to seeing tonight was David, Sr. He had been calling and leaving messages for months, telling me to back off my follow-up story on David, Jr. Of course, his persistent messages only fueled my desire to finish what I started. I had no idea how the evening would turn out, but I was pleased with the additional information I had already gathered from Victoria.

Darien

After Toni took Lil' Darien upstairs to finish his nap, I got up and checked my messages on my phone. I saw a text message from Vince. He said he wanted to talk and asked me to call him when I got a chance. I was still feeling a little conflicted about this situation between him and Toni. In my mind, I knew it was a long time ago and I shouldn't have anything to worry about. That was the rational side of my brain. The other side hated the very thought of him touching Toni in an intimate way. I couldn't bare the thought of it. It's so silly, but every time we're all together, I picture Toni naked and Vince touching her.

I missed my friend and the time we used to spend together. I had been through some major changes in the past year with getting married and becoming a father. I really needed someone to talk to about everything. So, I consulted with my mother of all people about my feelings about the situation. She had said, "Darien, you cannot fault that woman for who she slept with before you, just like she can't fault you. As many woman as you've been with over the years and as small as Harrisburg is, I'm sure if you dig deep enough you will find that you slept with one of her friends before, too." I had to admit she had a point, but I argued that the difference is I didn't have a child with one of her friends; well, at least I didn't think I did. Mama D shook her head and told me to pray about it, which was a foreign concept for me. I couldn't remember the last time I went to church or prayed to God for any reason. I didn't say this to my mom because I know how upset and disappointed she would be. She had raised me in the church and had expressed on several occasions how disappointed she was that I wasn't attending on a regular basis now.

I decided to return Vince's call right away. We had to talk through things, and the sooner the better. Vince's answered on the third ring.

"Hello," he said, sounding out of breath.

"Hey, Vince. I got your text asking me to call you. What's up, man?"

"First, I wanted to check to see how Toni is doing? She was pretty shaken up yesterday."

I was a little annoyed that the first thing he asked about was Toni, but I guess it made sense since she had fainted in the restaurant.

"She is doing much better," I replied.

"Good, I'm glad to hear that. Well, I wanted to talk to you and wondered if we could maybe meet for lunch or something, just the two of us."

"Yeah, I was thinking we should probably talk about things. So when do you want to meet?" I asked.

"I would really like to talk to you as soon as possible, so let me know when you're available," Vince responded.

I thought for a few seconds, wondering if I could meet him today before going to Jada's house tonight. Finally, I said, "Can you meet me this afternoon? We could meet at Your Place on Union Deposit."

Vince responded that he could meet me at two o'clock, and then we ended the call. I got up and went into the family room to tell Toni that I was going out to meet Vince for lunch. I found her writing in her journal. Sensing my presence as I entered the room, she closed her journal and turned towards me. I approached her and sat down next to her. I placed my hand on hers, which was resting on her knee.

"Darien, what's wrong, babe?" she asked with a look of concern in her eyes.

I smiled while looking at my beautiful wife, the mother of my son. I loved Toni so much, and I wished in that moment our paths could have crossed much sooner in our lives. None of this would be happening right now if that had been the case. Finally, I spoke.

"I just talked to Vince, and he and I would like to get together to talk."

I noticed Toni shift in her seat, a sign that she was nervous. I knew she sensed how uncomfortable I was with Vince since she revealed their prior relationship to me. We had several heated conversations about it over the past few months.

I squeezed her hand, looked into her eyes, and said, "Toni, I know I've had trouble dealing with all of this, and that's why it is so important that I go and talk to Vince now. I need my friend back, and the only way I can work towards that is to get my feelings out in the open. That's something I need to do one on one with Vince."

Toni nodded. "I understand, babe. Really I do. Just remember that we are supposed to be at Jada's house by six tonight."

"I know, and I promise I will be back in plenty of time to get ready for that."

I leaned in to give Toni a kiss, and then I went upstairs to prepare for my meeting with Vince. I had a little over an hour to prepare for our talk. I retired to my study upstairs, my think tank to compose my thoughts. I wanted this discussion to be productive, and I wanted to be able to express all of my feelings and concerns to Vince.

After spending about thirty minutes thinking about what to say to Vince, I finally got up and went into my room. I dressed quickly and headed out to meet Vince. As I drove down Union Deposit towards the restaurant, I began to feel a sense of relief. I hadn't even talked to Vince yet, but knowing what I wanted and needed to say was in itself a relief.

As I pulled into the parking lot, I saw Vince walking towards the restaurant. He noticed me pulling in, stopped walking, and waited for me to park. We met up at the door, gave each other a brief hug, and headed into the restaurant to talk.

Toni

God is good. Just as I was writing in my journal about how I wished Darien and Vince could get past all of this awkwardness, Darien came in to tell me that he and Vince were going to meet to talk. Once I heard Darien leave, I said a silent prayer that he and Vince have a productive discussion and come to terms with everything so the three of us can work together to raise Derrick and make him feel loved. I continued to write in my journal while Lil' Darien slept.

Tonight I'm going over to Jada's house for the memorial gathering for David, Jr. During this event, I'm supposed to reflect on him, and honestly, I'm having a little bit of trouble coming up with something positive to say. Now that I know about David and Gina, my entire perspective on David and Jada's relationship has changed. I always thought they had the perfect relationship, the perfect love. Jada always bragged about how they were each other's first and only. Well, of course now I knew that their love was anything but perfect and Jada certainly wasn't his only love. None of that mattered because Gina and I both agreed there was no point in bringing David's past to the light now. The only purpose it would serve would be causing pain for Jada.

I think for the gathering tonight I will focus on my view of their relationship and how it always inspired me. In addition, I will recount some of the funny stories we all shared from high school and college. Tonight, I want to see Jada smile again. It has been a year, so it's time for her to remember the good times. More importantly, it's now time for her to move on with her life.

Chapter 10

Vince

Darien and I grabbed a table and ordered a pitcher of beer. I couldn't believe how nervous I was sitting across from my best friend. Darien and I have known each other since we were kids, and here we were sitting in silence. This was nuts. I guess he was waiting for me to take the lead since I had contacted him about us getting together to talk. After clearing my throat, I began.

"Look, man, I know this is an awkward situation we're in right now."

He took a sip of his beer and nodded his head in agreement as I continued.

"You and I have been friends from way back, and early on we established the rule of not dating each others exes."

Darien shifted in his chair and looked around to see if anyone was within earshot of our conversation, but he didn't speak.

"I have thought about all of this, and I can only imagine how hard this must be for you. Especially now since we've confirmed that Derrick is mine. Darien, all I can tell you is that it was a long time ago, and Toni and I only dated briefly. We were not romantically involved for an extended period of time."

I paused to see if he would respond to anything I had said, but we only sat in silence for another minute or so.

"Darien, please say something."

Again, he shifted in his chair and took another sip of his beer before responding.

"I've thought about this situation, Vince, and I know all of what you just stated is true. Part of me, the rational part, understands all of it. I really do. However, there's the other part that still can't seem to get past it. Man, I love Toni, and the only reason I can handle thinking about her past is because it's not staring me in the face. As long as those other men she's been with are nameless and faceless, I can handle it. When I think about my best friend being intimate with my wife, I lose it."

As I listened to Darien, I knew exactly how he felt. It was a little different, but I knew what it felt like to love a woman so much you didn't want to imagine anyone else ever being near her in that way. I felt the same way for Gina once.

After taking a big gulp of my beer, I said, "Trust me, Darien, I understand all of that. But, I also know you're my best friend, and these past few months what I have been going through with Gina and not being able to talk to you about it, it's been hell, man. I wanted to talk to you today so we could determine how we can get past this so I can get my friend back. I'm fighting for custody of my son, an eight-year-old who I have never met, and I'm going to need my best friend to help me through this."

"Vince, I've missed our friendship as well over the past few months. I love Toni to death, but this marriage and father thing is rough for someone who vowed to be a bachelor until the day I die."

I laughed. Darien's last comment had helped ease some of the tension.

"Listen, man," he continued. "We're both going through some pretty heavy stuff right now, and we've been friends for as long as I can remember. We made the pact all those years ago never to date each other's exes, and up until this unfortunate twist of fate we never have. I trust you, and I trust my wife. I'm not going to lie. It's going to be tough, but I will make an effort to put my insecurities aside so we can go back to being friends and being there for each other. How does that sound?" Darien asked.

I smiled and lifted my mug. He lifted his, and we toasted to a truce. Things fell silent again for a few minutes. Darien appeared to be deep in thought.

"Darien? Hello, are you there?"

He shook his head yes and then responded, "Yes, I'm here. Sorry, I was just thinking."

"Well, I stopped talking a while ago, but you were just sitting there not saying anything. So, I was getting concerned about you."

He chuckled and took another sip of his beer. "No, man, I'm good. I was actually thinking about Derrick and how it's about him right now, not my feelings."

"Darien, you have no idea how much it means to me to hear you say that."

Darien laughed. "Okay, Vince, don't get all sappy on me. You have a son now, so you have to man up."

Now it was my turn to laugh. "Yeah, I know what you mean, man. You know I still haven't told my parents about any of this."

"Wow, man, I'm surprised. I thought you would have done that by now, especially since you know he's really yours."

"Yeah, I know, but I plan to tell them tomorrow afternoon. You know how I always go over for Sunday dinner."

"Yes, I do, and I miss those invitations to get some of that good food your mom makes."

I laughed and said, "Remember how we used to argue about whose mom made the best pies?"

"Yes, I remember that very well," Darien said with a chuckle. Then he asked,
"I almost hate to bring this up, but what's going on with you and Gina, man? Are you any closer to actually getting a divorce?"

"Man, that's a mess, but she did finally ask her daddy to help her out so she can buy me out of my half of the house."

"So she's going to keep the house, huh?"

"Yes, she is, and at this point, I really don't care as long as I get my half so I can start rebuilding my savings account. Boy am I mad I spent all that money on the wedding and then buying that house. I'm going to need some of that money to fund my Chicago move."

"So you really think that's what you're going to do?" Darien asked.

"Yeah. I think it'll be best for Derrick to keep him in familiar surroundings until he gets used to me being in his life."

With a look of concern, Darien said, "So, Vince, are you sure you're really through with Gina?"

I almost spit my beer out all over his face.

"I've never been so sure of anything in my life, man. There's no chance of reconciliation with her. My father always told me to know your bottom line, and for me, my bottom line is honesty. Gina crossed that line in the worse way possible."

Darien nodded while I spoke, which let me know he heard me loud and clear.

Finally, he said, "Well look, man, I have to run. Toni and I are going over to Jada's house tonight. I'm glad we got together and talked. Keep me posted on how your parents take the news and the ruling on custody."

I stood up and came around the table to give him a hug. After he left, I stayed a little while longer to finish the pitcher of beer and to pay the bill.

David, Sr.

As I drove towards Harrisburg, it seemed the closer I got, the more I wished I had not agreed to come. At first, visiting with Jada and the kids was a good distraction, but now it was too painful. Especially going to the house and seeing things just the way my son left them in his office. Part of me was glad Jada had not cleared out his things or tried to replace him, but on the other hand, the constant reminder or shrine she had for him was not healthy.

Jr. and I were very close, but after his mother died, our bond grew even stronger. Now that he was gone, I literally had no one. I spent twelve to fourteen hours each day at the office, including the weekends. I did whatever I could to avoid being in the house alone. I decided to discuss me spending more time with Tre and Jordan with Jada. They were the only things I had left in this world.

I shifted my thoughts to what I would say to everyone about my son's life. I would talk about how he gave back to the community with his coaching and mentoring. David always loved sports. He aspired to be a professional basketball player. When it became clear that wasn't going to happen, he was devastated. I remember the speech his mother gave him over the phone that night. She used the age-old adage 'when life throws lemons at you, make lemonade'. I smiled at the memory.

David was depressed for a while, but when he talked to his coach about it, he became inspired to give back by working with children to help them achieve their dreams. I feared he never thought I was proud of him because he didn't become a lawyer as I had hoped. I did push him hard, but in the end, I was very proud. I regret I never had a chance to tell him just how proud I was of him. He made a difference every day of his life by working with, inspiring, and encouraging youth. All I did all day long was try to keep people from going to jail, and most of the time, they were guilty as sin.

As I approached Jada's development, I took in the scenery around me. I considered for a moment if this would be somewhere I could retire one day. It would be great for me to be closer to spend time with my grandkids. Something else I could discuss with Jada when the time was right.

As I pulled up to the house, it appeared that I was the first to arrive. I parked and retrieved the flowers I had stopped to get for Jada. While walking towards the front door, I took notice that the house didn't look as well kept as it had when David was alive. I had gotten a cleaning company for Jada to keep the house clean inside, but it had not occurred to me to hire someone for the outside maintenance. I made a mental note to find someone to take care of the exterior of the house. I knew Jada had a lot on her plate. She insisted on going back to work full time, even though I offered to help so she could stay home or even start her own business. She refused, saying she needed to keep herself busy and had built a solid career that she did not want to walk away from.

I was feeling a little better about having come. It was going to be a great night hearing my son's wife and closest friends recount special times and share their stories. I was also going to get to see Tre and Jordan. I rang the doorbell and smiled while waiting for Jada to come to the door.

Toni

As Darien and I drove towards Jada's house after dropping Lil' Darien off with Mama D, I drilled him about his talk with Vince. When he came back home after meeting with him, he was in such a different mood, a good mood. I was curious how things went, but he didn't really seem interested in giving me the details. Instead, it seemed like he wanted to grill me on my relationship with Vince all those years ago. He also asked me for at least the tenth time today if Benjamin was coming to Jada's tonight.

I rolled my eyes as I answered, "Yes, Benjamin is going to be here tonight. I told you that this morning."

He shot me a 'don't start with me' look. My tone had been a little harsh, so I took a deep breath and asked him again about his talk with Vince.

"So you and Vince worked things out, huh?"

"I told you I really don't want to talk about it. Yes, we talked, and I feel a little better about the situation, but this is going to take some time."

I reached over and started stroking the back of his neck while he drove. I knew how much he loved that. It was my way of getting him to calm down and focus on something else.

"I understand, babe, and I'll let it go. I promise I will not ask about it again."

He looked at me and smiled. "That's why I love you so much. You know when to push and when to back off."

He was right. I had learned early on how to read him, so I knew when I was getting to his breaking point.

We rode in silence the rest of the way to Jada's house. I continued to stroke his neck, while he had his hand on my thigh. I thought to myself, *Damn, I love this man.*

Gina

As I drove to Jada's house, I was filled with nervous excitement. I called Susan's cell phone number. I hadn't heard from her since the email I sent about the story on David the other day.

"Hey, Gina," Susan answered. "What's going on?"

"Hey, I was just calling to see if you got my email about the follow-up story on David?

"Um, I didn't receive an email from you about that. I was just online going through my emails, and I don't have any emails from you."

"I know I sent it to you…" Just then, I realized I never sent the email because I had been interrupted by Toni's visit. "You know what, Susan. I typed up the email, but I never got a chance to send it because I got sidetracked."

"Okay, so what's the scoop? What was in the email?"

I don't know why, but something told me not to give Susan any details just yet. So, I said, "Well, I just wanted to let you know that I will have that follow-up story completed for you next week. I was finally able to get some of the other interviews completed."

Susan laughed. "Well, it's about time, don't you think? The man has been dead for a year now."

"I know, but trust me, you're going to like this article. It will be well worth the wait."

"Okay, I hope so. I know you really want a promotion, so I'm hoping this is the story that will give me the justification I need to go to bat for you."

"I really appreciate your support, and like I said, this is going to be a good one."

I ended the call just as I pulled up to Jada's house.

Chapter 11

Jada

After dropping the kids off at their respective destinations, I returned home and looked over everything one last time. The cleaning crew did a great job, as did the caterers. With everything in place, I was just waiting for my guests to arrive. I had avoided everyone's phone calls throughout the day. I had a message from Toni asking if I needed any help preparing for tonight, but I never responded to her. My mother even tried to call a few times to inquire about helping out. I had been thinking all day about how I would approach things, and I finally came up with a master plan. I thought to myself how everyone would react when Gina, my special guest, arrived.

The doorbell interrupted my thoughts. *My first guest has arrived, but who is it?* I thought to myself. I opened the door and there stood David, Sr. holding a beautiful flower arrangement.

"Hello, Sr.," I greeted as he walked past me towards the kitchen. "Please, just set those down on the counter. I'll take care of putting them on the table. So nice of you to bring those."

He did as I instructed and then came into the family room where I was waiting.

"Where is everyone else?"

"You're the first guest to arrive, but everyone else should be here very soon. My parents called and are just a few minutes away."

David, Sr. looked around a bit and then asked, "Where are the kids? I was hoping to see them again."

"They're spending the night with friends tonight. I didn't want them here, just in case I become very emotional again or something."

He nodded his head, indicating he understood. "So have you cleaned out his office?"

Shaking my head no, I responded, "Actually, I just went in there the other day after we went to the cemetery. I started to go through some things on his desk, but got discouraged quickly and decided to stop."

He stood up, walked over towards me, then sat down next to me and took my hand in his.

"I told you before I can do it for you. There's no reason for you to worry yourself with all of that stuff. Jr. and I worked very closely together, so I'm sure there is nothing in there that I don't already know about."

I thought, *Okay, now is my chance to ask.*

So, I cleared my throat and said, "Funny you should say that. I was wondering if you knew anything about David, Jr. and a woman named Gina?"

Sr. looked like I had just punched him in his stomach. He started to respond, but the doorbell rang again. I pulled my hand away from his and walked towards the door.

As I walked away from him, I said, "We'll talk more about that later."

When I opened the door, I saw my parents as well as Benjamin standing there. I invited everyone in and offered them a chance to get something to drink while we waited for the remaining guests to arrive. I paid attention to how Benjamin interacted with David, Sr. I hadn't noticed before tonight how their interaction seemed a bit strained. I also looked at Benjamin differently. I had this overwhelming desire to give him a big hug but stopped myself, because once I went there, all of my emotions would come out. Everyone milled around in the family room chit-chatting while I busied myself in the kitchen checking on the food.

I thought I had done a great job of keeping up a good appearance, until my mother walked into the kitchen and cornered me.

"What's going on, Jada? I've been trying to reach you all day. You clearly have been avoiding my calls. Then I get here and you look a hot mess."

I was offended by her comment. Even though I barely had two hours of sleep last night, I thought I had done a pretty good job of pulling myself together, but obviously not. *It's hard to fool your mother*, I thought to myself.

"Mom, I'm fine. Just a little emotionally drained right now. The past few days have been difficult. Getting everything ready for tonight was very exhausting, also."

My mother's face softened as she walked towards me and gave me a nice hug.

"I know, baby. This week has probably been very difficult for you, but please don't shut me out. I became really worried when I couldn't reach you earlier today."

"I'm sorry, Ma. I promise I'll do a better job of keeping in touch with you since I know how you worry."

Just then, the doorbell rang again, and I assumed it was Toni. I left my mother standing in the kitchen to answer the door. It was in fact Toni and Darien. I showed them in and directed them into the family room.

My mother had rejoined the group in the family room. It appeared that everyone assumed it was time to get started since Toni had arrived. After getting everyone's attention, I informed them that we were waiting for another guest who would be arriving shortly. As I spoke, Toni and a few others looked around with perplexed looks on their faces. I knew they were trying to determine who the guest would be.

"Everyone, please go ahead and grab something to eat and drink while we wait on our special guest."

Toni stood up and walked over towards me with a confused look on her face. I had no intentions on letting her in on my secret, but I knew she was going to try to get it out of me.

"Jada," she said, drawing closer to me, "what's going on?"

I rolled my eyes and sighed heavily before responding, "What do you mean?"

She sucked her teeth. "Don't be cute with me. You know exactly what I mean. What's with the mystery guest?"

"Toni, please just go get some food and take your seat in the family room. Don't start anything with me tonight. I am not in the mood, trust me."

Toni stepped back and looked me up and down like she couldn't believe the attitude I was giving her. It was completely out of character for me to speak to her this way, but seriously, I was not in the mood. I wanted this night to be over so I could move on. Toni slowly backed away while keeping her eyes on me until I turned and walked the other way.

I glanced at my watch to check the time. I had purposely told Gina to come approximately forty-five minutes after everyone else to ensure she would be the last to arrive. My decision to track her down and invite her was twofold. One, I wanted to corner her to find out exactly what was going on between her and my husband. This part she didn't know about. The second reason, which is how I lured her here, was so she could record for her follow-up article everyone's reflections about David.

Right on cue, the doorbell rang, and I knew it was Gina. As I went to the door, all eyes in the room followed me. When Gina and I walked into the room, Toni and Darien almost spit out their food. No one else in the room flinched. The reaction to seeing Gina was key, as I wanted to know if David, Sr. knew anything about her. He didn't seem to, which made me feel a little better. Toni gave me a strange look and mouthed to me, *What is she doing here?* I simply smiled and offered Gina a seat. Standing in the middle of my family room, I formally introduced Gina to everyone.

"Everyone, this is Gina. She's a reporter and was a close friend of David, Jr.'s."

I noticed David, Sr. adjust himself a bit in his chair. My parents and Benjamin didn't react at all. Benjamin was too busy watching Toni out of the side of his eye, and Darien had his eye on him, too. Toni just looked confused.

"I invited Gina here tonight so she can finish her story on David's life. She interviewed him a few years ago and has been trying to do a follow-up story ever since his death." Turning to Benjamin, I said, "Benjamin, I believe Gina has been trying to contact you over the past year to interview you for her story, also. Hopefully, you can give her what she needs tonight so she can complete her article."

Benjamin nodded his head, but I could tell he was not comfortable with talking to her. He quickly turned to David, Sr., as if looking for his permission to speak.

David, Sr. stood up and walked towards me. In a hushed voice, he said, "Jada, are you okay? This doesn't seem like you."

I responded a little louder than I intended. "I'm fine. Now please sit back down so we can get this over with."

I noticed everyone looking around at each other now. I had to hold it together or else this could be a disaster. Taking a deep breath, I counted to ten to control my emotions. Then, I continued.

"Okay, everyone is here. So, let's get started. We're all gathered here today to remember and reflect on the life of my late husband, David Wright, Jr. I would like to ask David, Sr. to get us started with his reflection on Jr.'s life."

When he stood up, Gina pulled a notepad out of her purse to start taking notes.

"As I drove here tonight, knowing I had to come up with one special thing to say about my son, I became overcome with emotion, so much so that I had to pull over at one point to gather myself. Most of you in this room know how very close Jr. and I were to each other. Back in the old neighborhood when Jr. was a young boy, the neighbors would tease us about Jr. being my shadow. You wouldn't see one of us without the other. But, this is supposed to be about his life and what I think he made of it. Honestly, I was very disappointed when he decided not to follow in my footsteps. Every father wants their son to grow up to be like them or better. When he chose sports, I was devastated beyond words. My late wife, David's mother, helped me through it by reminding me that it was his life to live, and as long as he was happy, I should let it be. My son touched the lives of many young people in his role as coach and athletic director. So, all in all, I feel good about his life, the mark he left on his beautiful family, and all the lives he touched over the years."

By the time he finished, there wasn't a dry eye in the room. Even Gina seemed moved by David, Sr.'s comments.

Next to speak was Benjamin, who recounted several funny stories of the good ole days when he and David were growing up in Greenbelt, Maryland, and playing basketball together at the recreation center in Spring Hill Lake. Toni followed Benjamin and added some stories of her own from high school and college, which had everyone laughing. My parents both stood up and made brief comments.

Then it was my turn. All eyes were on me. I had been thinking about this all day, and now that my moment had arrived, I was at a loss for words. I closed my eyes and pictured the words from the letters I had stayed up all night reading. Tears began to form in my eyes. I opened them and looked around the room. First to Benjamin, then Toni, and finally David, Sr. I wiped my eyes and began to address my friends and family.

"Mom, Dad, David, Sr., Toni, and Benjamin, I appreciate you all being here with me tonight as we celebrate and remember the life of my late husband David Jr. As you all know, David was my world. He was my first and only love. I never regretted one minute of my life together with him…until last night."

I watched as Toni and the others started looking around the room at each other as they tried to understand my last remark.

"You see, up until last night, I believed with all of my heart and soul that my marriage was solid and built on trust and honesty."

Toni stood up, interrupting me. "Jada, what are you talking about?"

I put up my hand to silence her. "Toni, please sit down and let me finish. In fact, everyone please let me get this out without interrupting me."

Toni and my mother were sitting on the edge of their seats. Toni started wringing her hands, which is something she did when she was nervous. Darien, who looked concerned, had his arm around her waist.

I cleared my throat and continued. "First, I have to apologize to Benjamin. Benjamin, for the past year, I have treated you like something less than a human being. We were once such close friends. You were always such a nice, caring, and giving person. Yet, somehow over the years, I forgot about that part of you, or I would have never allowed myself to believe the lies I was being told about you."

Benjamin smiled a nervous smile at me, but looked confused. I noticed David Sr. getting very uncomfortable as he looked at Toni and Benjamin with red-hot anger in his eyes. I saw this and figured he thought they had let the cat out of the bag. I decided to address him next.

"David, Sr., your reflection was very nice, but you left something out, didn't you?"

David, Sr. looked around the room like he had no idea what I was referring to.

I walked over to him, put my hand on his shoulder, and said, "Didn't you forget to mention how you ran behind David, Jr. using your wealth and power to clean up his messes? Oh, and to make sure others took the fall for him."

David jumped up out of his seat and lunged at Benjamin. "How could you?" he shouted. "You swore you would never tell Jada the truth. I'm going to kill you."

Darien and my father ran over to pull David, Sr. off of Benjamin. While everyone was distracted, I reached under the table and pulled out the box of letters.

"No one told anything!" I screamed at the top of my lungs. "I read it all for myself in these letters I found in David's office last night. The letters that Benjamin wrote to Toni from jail"

Everyone stopped and looked at me. At this point, I must have looked a complete mess. I was crying so hard I could barely see. My mother ran over to me and grabbed the box of letters. At the same time, Toni came towards me and tried to hug me, but I pushed her back.

"Don't touch me. I know you knew about this for the past year, and you didn't tell me either."

Toni backed away. "But, Jada, I..."

I put my hand up, letting her know I didn't want to hear it. As she sat back down, she covered her mouth and started to cry. Darien ran to her side and embraced her.   David Sr. just sat on the couch with his head in his hands, shaking it back and forth. I wasn't done yet, though.

Next, I turned to Gina and said, "So, Gina, why don't you give your reflection now?"

Gina shook her head. "No, Jada, I don't have anything to say."

I was getting really angry now. "Oh really?" I said, walking towards her. "Well, why don't you at least explain why you were meeting my husband for lunch two to three times a week over the period of several months early last year?"

Gina's eyes almost popped out of her head. She stood up and began to gather her things. "I don't know what you're trying to do here, but I'm leaving. Forget about the article. You all have some issues to work out."

Just as she started to head towards the door, I grabbed her shoulder and spun her around to face me.

"Don't walk away from me now. You're here in my house with my friends and family. Now, tell me the truth."

Gina looked towards Toni like she was pleading for her help, but Toni shook her head no. Quickly, I ran towards Toni and smacked her across the face.

"You knew about her being with David and you didn't tell me?" I screamed.

Both Toni and Darien jumped up. Toni grabbed her face where I had hit her.

"Jada, I know you're upset," Darien said, "but I am not going to stand here and let you hit my wife again. This is getting out of control. Everyone needs to sit down and calm down right now."

Everyone sat down except for Benjamin. Out of the corner of my eye, I saw him get up from his seat and walk towards me. It seemed like it was happening in slow motion. Everyone including David Sr. just sat in their seats and watched him. He didn't say a word; he just grabbed me and hugged me. He held me for what seemed like hours, and I felt myself melt in his arms. The lack of sleep and the roller coaster ride of emotions from the past few days had finally caught up with me.

After a few minutes, he whispered softly in my ear, "Jada, I loved you and David, and I did what I thought was the best thing for everyone at the time. I'm so sorry I caused you any pain. I never meant to do that."

I pulled myself back from his embrace and looked him in his eyes. "Benjamin, you have nothing to be sorry about. You are my hero."

I had let things get way out of control. My mother finally decided she'd had enough, so she stood up and addressed the guests.

"Okay, I think it's time for everyone to go home. Obviously, there is a lot for everyone to think about as they drive home tonight. My daughter is distraught, and I would appreciate it if everyone would leave now."

Out of the corner of my eye, I saw Gina stand up. Tears were streaming down her cheeks, and she raised her hand like she wanted to say something.

"Mom, please let Gina speak," I managed to say.

My mother turned to Gina and nodded.

Gina cleared her throat before she began speaking. "I didn't come here tonight to do this. I came because Jada invited me to participate so I could finish my story about David's life. Well, I can't finish his story without writing about his little girl, Samantha, who he will never know."

There was a collective gasp from everyone in the room. Even I gasped at that admission. I figured they had an affair, but had no idea there was a child involved, too.

David Sr. jumped up and ran towards her with outstretched arms. "I have another grandchild?"

Gina nodded her head yes.

Darien turned to Toni and said, "You were right, babe."

My mother came to my side to console me, or maybe it was to ensure I didn't go after Gina. I had no desire to attack Gina; she was not the person I was upset or angry with right now. It was my husband. I couldn't believe he had negatively impacted so many people's lives this way. I had him up on a pedestal for so long, it was hard to believe the man I loved so deeply had lied and betrayed me and others for so long. I found myself asking who he was. How could I have slept in the same bed with someone like this?

I sat down on the couch and completely lost it. My mother was torn between whether she should come to my side to console me or help my guests out the door. The only guest who did not move was David, Sr. Through my tears, I saw him whispering something to my parents. Then he came back and sat down. With just the four of us remaining, David Sr. stood up and began to speak.

"Jada, I know you're very upset right now, and I realize a lot of your pain was caused by my actions. Yes, I was trying to protect my son, but I was also trying to protect you. Jada, I love you like a daughter. My son made a horrible mistake, and it was selfish of me to trade another man's life for my son's. Please forgive me."

The entire time David Sr. was talking more and more anger was building up inside of me. I wanted to jump up and wring his neck. How could he be apologizing to me? What about all the others' lives he ruined in the process? When he finished, we sat in silence for a few minutes while I collected my thoughts and myself. My mother handed me the box of tissue, and I blew my nose before addressing David Sr.

When I was finally ready, I said, "I'm not the one you should be apologizing to. What about everyone else who was affected by your scheming and conniving lies?"

"Jada, I..."

I put my hand up to silence him. "I'm sorry. Sr., but you need to leave my house right now. I don't have anything further to say to you right now."

He started backing away from me, but his arms were still outstretched towards me. I saw the tears falling from his eyes, and although I hate to see a grown man cry, I wasn't fazed by his display of emotion. I was mad as hell and just wanted him out of my face. As he backed towards the front door, he continued to plead with me.

"Jada, please, just hear me out. Jada, please."

I kept shaking my head and motioning for him to leave.

Through all of this drama, my father had remained quiet, but now as David, Sr. headed out, I saw my father shaking his head and I could hear him mumbling something about never trusting any of them in the first place. My mother shushed my father because even though he was right in his initial assessment of Sr. and my husband, now was not the time for 'I told you so'.

Standing up, I headed towards the stairs. I was a mess; I needed a nice, long soak in my tub and a good night's sleep. I knew my mother understood exactly because she did not say a word as I started up the stairs.

Chapter 12

Toni

Once Darien and I were outside, we saw Gina and Benjamin standing together near their cars. I headed towards them, motioning for Darien to follow me. I wanted to go over to speak to them. As we approached, I could tell Benjamin was very agitated by the expression on his face. Gina looked as if she was pleading with him, and as I drew closer, she stopped talking.

Once I was close enough to whisper so they could both hear me, I asked, "What are you two talking about now?"

They both looked at each other for a moment, and then Benjamin said, "Gina was just filling me in on the story she's planning to run in the local paper about David and the girl from college."

I looked from Benjamin to Gina and then replied, "Gina, what is Benjamin talking about? You didn't mention anything to me about this when we spoke the other day."

Darien stepped up closer and chimed in, "You spoke to Gina the other day? About what?"

I turned to Darien and said, "That's not really important right now. You and I can discuss it later."

By his facial expression and body language, I could tell he was not happy with my answer. I would deal with him later. Right now, I needed to get more information about this story.

"So, Gina," I continued, "tell me about this story and why you feel you need to tell this part of David's life now."

Gina seemed like she was losing her patience. She closed her eyes, tilted her head up, and then let out a heavy sigh before finally answering.

"Look, I'm a journalist; writing stories is what I do. Ever since David died, my editor has been on my case about doing a follow-up story on his life."

I interrupted her. "Okay, I can understand that, but please tell me how bringing this issue out is going to help. Think about it, Gina. Your daughter is David's child. Would you want her to one day read about how her father raped and beat some young girl?"

Gina gasped and grabbed her chest. Tears started flowing as she said, "No, I would never want my daughter to read such horrible things about her father. That's not the point of the story. The story is to allow Victoria to tell the truth about what really happened. David didn't rape her."

"Who is Victoria?"

"The girl who was involved in the incident with David," Gina responded.

"That may be true that he didn't rape her, but he still beat her so badly that she ended up in a coma for over a month."

I could tell Gina had not considered that piece of the story. She started looking for her keys in her purse, and once she found them, she started backing away.

"I need to go," she simply said. "I can't talk about this anymore tonight. There is just too much. I…I have to go now."

Darien, Benjamin, and I just stood there and watched as Gina got into her car and pulled off. Darien finally spoke, breaking the silence in the air.

"Come on, Toni. Let's go pick up Lil' Darien." He put his arm around me and started pulling me towards our car.

My eyes locked with Benjamin's, but neither of us said a word. He simply turned and started walking towards his car.

Once inside the car, Darien and I sat there in complete silence for a few minutes. Finally, he said, "Well, at least everything is out in the open now, huh?"

I was still in shock. I never wanted Jada to find out about David cheating on her. That was the whole reason I went to meet with Gina, but I didn't want Darien to know I had done that. The part about her finding out it was David and not Benjamin who attacked the girl didn't bother me. Since David was now dead, it didn't really matter. I was just glad Benjamin's name had been cleared. I wondered what was in those letters that she found. I managed to snatch one off the floor during all of the chaos and couldn't wait to read it.

"Yes, finally everything is out in the open," I responded to Darien's comment. "Even though she's upset with me right now, she'll come around. Maybe now she can really start to heal and start her life over."

"So now we know who Gina's baby belongs to," Darien said.

"Yes, we do. Are you going to say anything to Vince about it?" I asked.

Darien thought for a minute and finally said, "I'm not sure yet. Vince has a lot on his plate right now, and I don't think he needs this distraction. Besides, Gina should be the one to tell him, not me."

I nodded my head in agreement.

After starting the ignition, Darien turned to me and said, "We better get over to Mama D's to pick up Lil' Darien before it gets too much later."

I agreed, and we were on our way. As Darien drove, I was thankful he didn't press me about why I had met with Gina the other day. I hoped that he forgot about it and would not bring it up again. I thought about the letter I was hiding in my jacket. I wish I could read every one of the letters Benjamin wrote me, but I would have to settle for having just this one.

Gina

As I drove away from Jada's house, Toni's words kept playing in my head. She was right; how could I publish such damaging information about David and not realize the impact it would have on Samantha? I also thought about the fact that now that David, Sr. knew about his granddaughter, he would want to have a relationship with her. My story would affect him, as well. It might even cause him to lose his license or his practice. The more I thought about everything, the more I realized I couldn't run the story about Victoria. Thank goodness I didn't actually send that email to Susan. Now I had to come up with something just as good so Susan would be happy. I also had to think about how to let Victoria know I had changed my mind about publishing her story. I would deal with that on Monday.

Benjamin

As I drove south on I-83, I felt such a sense of relief. Even though I knew Jada was hurting, it was a relief to have everything out in the open. I smiled to myself as I remembered the look on Toni's face as she grabbed one of the letters Jada had thrown and stuffed it in her pocket. I wanted her to read them all so she could know how much I loved and missed her all those years we were apart. I watched how she and Darien interacted with each other tonight, and it appeared their love and bond was solid. Even if Toni did read every letter I wrote, in the end, I'm sure it would not make a difference. The reality is she has moved on and has built a new life with Darien. Now I needed to let the past go and do the same thing.

I switched gears for a minute and thought about David, Sr., who looked defeated after everything had come out. I really shouldn't care one bit about him or his feelings after the way he treated me, but I still looked up to and respected him. He took me in after my mother died and made sure I had a good life. I did wonder if he would ever get around to apologizing to me for taking away seven good years of my life and causing me to lose the love of my life.

Shaking my head, I said aloud, "Don't hold your breath, Benjamin. He's way too proud for that."

An image came into my head of Jada crying. Seeing the pain and sadness in her eyes was too much for me to take. That's why I got up and went over to her. I couldn't believe she melted in my arms the way she did. I guess once she read those letters, all of her anger and hostility towards me was washed away. I knew she would need some time and space to deal with everything, but I also knew we would need to talk again. I'm sure she would eventually want to know the details regarding the incident involving David and the girl, and I knew she would come to me for answers. I also had some questions, but since David, Jr. was gone, they would remain unanswered.

Needless to say, I was as surprised as everyone else to find that David had cheated on Jada with Gina and had another child.

David Sr.

The walk from the front door to my car seemed to take forever. My head was pounding, and tears were still streaming down my face as I made my way to the driver's side and unlocked the door. While sitting in the car, I tried to collect my thoughts before starting the ignition. Finally, I felt comfortable and started the car. As I drove away from Jada's house, I couldn't help but think this might be the last time I visited her.

The day I always dreaded had come. Jada knew about David's infidelity and the violent attack. Actually, it was much worse than I even knew. I was in total shock about Gina and her child Samantha. I was Mr. Fix It, but this was a situation even I couldn't figure a way to fix. Jada felt betrayed by both my son and myself. I knew there was nothing I could do to repair the damage already done by her finding out the truth this way. I would have to give her time and space to sort her feelings out.

As I drove, I thought about Gina and my other grandchild. Even though this was a horrible situation with Gina being my deceased son's mistress, I wanted to connect with her and meet my other grandchild. Family was very important to me. Keeping my family intact was the main reason I got involved with things the way I did. Since it seemed I might have lost Tre and Jordan, I needed to meet and establish a relationship with Gina and Samantha right away. I also needed to work on revising my will to include Samantha. These were all things I would take care of on Monday as soon as I got to the office. In addition, I made a mental note to check on Victoria to make sure she was keeping up her end of the bargain. The last thing I needed would be for her to show up and stir things up even more with Jada about the attack.

Jada

While I undressed and started my bath, I could hear my parents getting into a heated discussion about the evening's events. I heard my father say,

"I cannot believe all of these people lying and cheating. I told Jada not to marry that man in the first place." I thought to myself that I couldn't even blame him at this point for what he said, he was right but my mother quickly interrupted him and said,

"Larry, now is not the time for all those 'I told you so' speeches." I heard my father try to interrupt, "Julia, I..." I couldn't see them but I knew my mother well and I imagined that she put her hand up to silence him and then she continued.

"Larry, I'm serious. Our daughter is going through some serious drama right now. We all know you were right about David, Jr. and his people, but now is not the time to bring it up. Our baby, Jada lost her husband a year ago, and just when she was coming to terms with that, she finds out he committed a horrible crime, cheated on her, and had another child. Don't you think that's enough for her to deal with right now?" I heard my father let out a heavy sigh and then he said,

"Yes Julia, you are right. Jada needs our support now more than ever. I will do my best to let things go, but if David, Sr. comes around here again with that sob story of he did it out of love for her, all bets are off." Hearing my mother explain exactly how I was feeling made me feel closer to her than I had felt in a very long time and hearing my father getting so worked up and ready to defend me made me smile even though I was crying and feeling so much pain and hurt inside.

I finished undressing and slid into my warm bubble bath to soak all my troubles away. As I replayed the events of the night in my head, I wanted to cry, but there were no more tears left. I felt numb and I had no idea what my next move was going to be. I felt I had been betrayed by everyone I was close to and there was no one to turn to. At this point I just wanted someone to hold me and tell me that everything would be okay. I must have drifted off to sleep, because the next thing I remember was my mother gently tapping my shoulder and telling me to get out of the tub.

Toni

We arrived at Mama D's house, and Darien rushed inside to get Lil' Darien. I was so mentally exhausted that I started to fall asleep during the ride to his mother's house. While he was in the house, I retrieved the hidden letter and tried to read it, but it was too dark and Darien returned in less than five minutes with Lil' Darien, who was still wide awake. Darien's mood had changed.

Noticing he was very upset, I asked him, "Babe, what's wrong?"

As he continued to get Lil' Darien loaded into the car, he mumbled, "Joy is up to her old tricks again. She and Mama got into an argument earlier, and she left and hasn't come back yet."

I shook my head in disbelief as Darien continued.

"Mama's not feeling well. I'm sure it's the stress from all this fighting and bickering with Joy."

I hated when Darien got like this. He always got himself worked up and irritated when Joy fought with his mom. I had to admit Joy was a handful. She never wanted to follow the rules and seemed to get mixed up with the wrong crowd all the time.

"What's wrong with Mama D?" I asked as Darien got into the driver's seat and started the car.

"She didn't say anything was wrong, but I can tell when she's not feeling well."

"Babe, maybe she's just tired. You know taking care of Lil' Darien is a rough job for us, and we're not as old as your mother."

Darien chuckled. "I know, right? That little boy is a bundle of energy, and all he wants to do is eat."

Now it was my turn to laugh.

"So what about Joy? Are you going to look for her after you take us home?"

Darien sighed heavily and replied, "No. Mama D told me not to worry about it. She said she knew where she was and that she would come back home in a few hours. I'll come over tomorrow morning to check on her and to make sure Joy came home."

As he drove, I started stroking the back of his neck to calm him down.

When we arrived at our house, Darien brought Lil' Darien in while I went to the kitchen to prepare his nighttime bottle. We met in the nursery, and I told Darien to go ahead and get ready for bed. I would handle putting Lil' Darien down for the night, even though it was his turn. On the weekends, Darien and I took turns putting Lil' Darien down for the night and taking the first shift. Lil' Darien still woke up every three to four hours for a bottle. Even though I was still at home, Darien liked to let me sleep in on the weekends since he didn't have to go to work.

After dressing Lil' Darien in his sleeper, I sat in the rocking chair and fed him his bottle. Once he was fed, burped, and fast asleep, I put him down in the crib and returned to the rocking chair, where I took the letter out of my pocket and started to read it.

Dear Toni,

It has been six months, and whoever said it gets easier as each day passes was telling a lie. I keep writing to you every week as I promised I would, but I'm getting very concerned because I have not heard back from you. I do hope you're not upset with me for making this choice. I know it's hard on you, but I did what I felt was best for everyone involved. Jada and David have a child, and that child needs both parents right now.

116

I do have a little bit of bad news. My first appeal was denied, so I have to start the process all over again. David Sr. is being very helpful. He's paying for everything and trying to get me the best lawyers he can on my defense team. Don't be discouraged. I'm sure David Sr. will find a way to get me out of here sooner than the seven years I was sentenced. You and I just have to be patient and have faith that everything will work out. Remember the saying that people come into your life for a reason, a season, or for a lifetime. Well, Toni, you are in my life for life. Please don't give up on me, and please write me back. I need to know that you are okay and that you are waiting for me.

I was moved to tears by what I read. Benjamin had poured his heart out to me and begged me to wait for him. I immediately became angry with David for keeping these letters from me all these years. I had been alone in Chicago while Benjamin was alone in jail, locked up for a crime he didn't commit. His only friend, David, was supposed to let me in on his whereabouts, but decided to keep that information to himself.

I didn't realize I was sobbing until Darien, who stood at the door of the nursery, asked me what was wrong. Since I hadn't heard him coming, I didn't have time to hide the letter from Benjamin. He walked over to me and took it from my hand. I tried to keep it from him, but he took it and walked out of the room. I gathered my things and followed him. When I entered our bedroom, he was sitting on the side of the bed reading the letter. I decided to let him finish before saying anything.

When he finally finished, he asked, "Toni, are you still in love with him?"

I knelt down on my knees in front of Darien and laid my head on his lap, but he pulled my head up so he could look into my eyes. He took his thumb and wiped my tears away.

"Toni, please answer me."

Sniffling, I replied, "Darien, I love you."

"I know you love me, Toni, but I need to know if you still love Benjamin, too."

117

Long before the words came out, I was shaking my head no. I finally managed to say, "No, I don't love Benjamin."

He leaned forward and kissed my forehead. "So why are you crying?"

"I'm crying tears of sorrow and joy. I'm crying tears of sorrow over the love I lost with Benjamin, and I'm crying tears of joy for the love I have with you."

Darien pulled me up to him, gently kissed my lips, and said, "Another thing I love about you is that you always say the right thing."

Darien lay back on the bed and pulled me to him so I could rest my head on his chest. I thought about Darien's question about me loving Benjamin. I said no, but deep down, I knew I still had unresolved feelings for Benjamin. Reading his letter brought back so many memories.

Mentally exhausted, we laid in silence, both lost in our own thoughts until we drifted off to sleep.

Darien

The sound of Lil' Darien crying awakened me. I looked over at the clock, and he was right on schedule; it was three o'clock in the morning. I looked over at Toni, who was sound asleep. She'd had a very emotionally draining day and needed her rest, so I decided not to disturb her.

I tended to Lil' Darien's needs and returned to my bedroom to find Toni in the exact same position she was in when I left. Standing by her side, I watched her sleep for a while. I really loved Toni. Most men would be concerned about Benjamin coming back into the picture, but for some reason, I was not concerned about him at all. I believed Toni when she said she was no longer in love with him. Since the very beginning, she had been nothing but honest with me, and I felt she had no reason to start being dishonest with me now.

After climbing in bed next to my wife, I drifted back to sleep.

Gina

I was prepared to stay up all night if I had to in order to rewrite the follow-up article about David's life. Pulling out my original article, I used it for inspiration and reference. I smiled as I remembered David during our first few meetings. He tried to keep everything professional, but clearly, there was an attraction between us. Eventually, he stopped fighting it, and we started seeing each other on a regular basis.

Even though he cheated on his wife and had a violent confrontation while drunk in college, I still believed he was a decent man, and I planned to write an article that would honor him so all of his children could grow up and be proud. I decided that since I had focused so much on his work with the children in the first story, I would use some of what David, Sr. talked about earlier before things got out of control. I would talk about his close relationship with his father and the reason why he decided to work with children. In addition, I would talk about his special relationship with Benjamin. In the end, I think everyone will be happy with what finally ends up in print.

Chapter 13

Vince

I was very nervous as I headed over early to my parents' house. I normally go for dinner around four o'clock, but today, I decided to go over right after church. Another good habit I had picked up since the split from Gina was going back to church. I even considered joining the men's Bible Study group and possibly volunteering to play for the choir sometimes. However, I didn't want to over commit to anything since I had no idea how things were going to turn out in the custody case.

As I pulled up to my parents' house, I became even more nervous. I sat in the car for a minute and collected my thoughts. Then I looked at my surroundings and thought about my childhood while growing up in the neighborhood. I thought about all of the special times with my dad, playing ball or just sitting on the porch eating ice cream and talking to him. I wanted my son Derrick to have those kinds of pleasant memories of his childhood. Not courtrooms and custody battles.

I must have been sitting in the car longer than I thought, because the next thing I knew my mother was standing at the door waving for me to come inside.

I waved back, got out of the car, and walked up to the door, where she was waiting to open it for me.

"Hey Ma," I said, walking inside. "How are you today?" I hugged her and gave her a quick peck on the cheek.

She responded, "I'm doing well, son. What took you so long to get out of the car? What were you doing in there?"

Just then, my father came around the corner fussing.

"Oh, Evie, leave that boy alone. You're always up in his business."

As I walked to the family room, both of my parents followed me. My father had the game on the TV, and I walked over to turn it off, which I knew would get a reaction out of him.

Right on cue, he said, "Hey, son, what are you doing? The Eagles have the ball."

I walked over to the chair I always sat in next to my father's and took a seat. My father and mother had concerned looks on their faces. My mother sat down on the sofa and motioned for my father to sit, as well. Once everyone was seated, I started.

"Mom and Dad, I have something very important to talk to you about today."

My mother rose up in her seat until she was right on the edge. "What is it, son? Are you in trouble?"

I smiled at my mother to help ease her mind, and it must have worked because she seemed to relax a bit when she saw me smiling.

"I'm fine, Ma. I just need to tell you both something."

"Well, go ahead, son, and tell us so I can get back to watching the game," my dad said.

My mom sucked her teeth, shot him an angry look, and then said, "Victor, that game is not more important than your son. So, hush and let him talk to us."

In order to keep the peace, I decided to get right to it.

Taking a deep breath, I told them, "Mom, Dad, I recently found out that I have a son."

My mom gasped. "What? When did this...? Who is she? Where is he?"

I put my hand up to stop her and continued. "Let me get through telling you everything I know and then you can ask me any questions you have."

I explained everything to my parents about my brief relationship with Toni. They were shocked to find out that Toni was Darien's wife. They didn't understand why she wouldn't tell me about the baby, so I explained about Benjamin and the fact that she said she tried to find me but was unable to. I also filled them in on the paternity test and the custody battle with Derrick's adoptive parents. When I finished, my mother was in tears, and my father shook his head in disbelief.

"Son, are you sure you know what you're doing?" my father asked. "Taking on an eight-year-old boy all alone is a lot."

Mom chimed in. "Victor, he's not going to be doing it alone. We're going to help him."

Mom's response made me smile.

"Dad, Mom is right. There's no way I can do this without some help. I told the judge that I would be willing to move to Chicago at least temporarily while Derrick and I get to know each other. That way, we can spend time together in his familiar surroundings. Nothing is set in stone yet, though. I have another three or four weeks before I will know what his initial ruling is on the custody case."

"Have you met him yet?" my mother asked. "What does he look like?"

"No, I haven't met him yet. He has been through so much already that I didn't want to confuse things even more until the court makes a decision on custody. As for what he looks like, my attorney will be sending pictures to me this week."

I could tell my mother was excited about having a grandchild, while my father seemed a little bit more reserved and cautious about it. I answered a few more questions for my mom, and then she went into the kitchen to finish preparing dinner. After she left the room, my father took the opportunity to turn the TV back on to catch up on the game.

After watching the game for a few minutes, he turned to me and said, "Son, you've been through a lot this year—a wedding, preparing for the birth of a baby only to discover it wasn't your baby. Are you sure you're seeking custody of this child because it is what's best for him and not what you need right now?"

I thought long and hard about how to answer my father. We let the question and silence hang between us for a while.

Once I had carefully thought about my response, I said, "Dad, I understand how you could feel that this is about me and trying to gain back what I lost. I actually asked myself that same question. At first, it was just about me finding out if the child was mine. Yes, I was motivated by the hurt and pain of what Gina put me through, but after I found out about his current situation, even before the DNA test confirmed he was mine, I decided I had to do something to help ease some of his pain. Even now, I am concerned about how coming into his life might affect him. I have been in contact with the counselor he's been seeing, and she's the one who suggested I wait to meet him until the court rules on the custody case."

I could tell by my father's body language that he was pleased with my answer. He seemed to relax a bit and sit back in his chair.

"So when do we get to meet our grandson?" he asked.

I smiled and got up to give my father a hug.

Dinner was great. Both my mother and father were very excited. My mother even asked my father about them traveling with me for the custody hearing next month.

As I drove home from my parents' house, I felt content, something I hadn't felt in a long time. I was very anxious to move forward with getting to know my son and building a relationship with him. I needed to map out my strategy for being able to handle the responsibility of a child.

When I got home, I sat down and created a list of all of the things I needed to take care of. First on my list was contacting Greg to see if I could pick up any studio work with him in Chicago. I also wanted to check into getting a small place out there since I would be going back and forth frequently. Now that my parents were aware, and clearly my mom was on board with doing whatever she could to help, it seemed that things were falling into place. I added talking to Jada about having the boys meet to my list of things to do, also.

Chapter 14

Darien

After breakfast, I got ready to head over to Mama D's house to check on things. I called when I first woke up this morning, but didn't get an answer. I picked up Lil' Darien kissed him, then walked over to Toni and gave her a hug and kiss before heading out the door.

As I drove down Lingelstown Road towards Front Street, I thought about how I planned to handle my sister Joy. She was a typical teenager, but she was stressing my mother out, and I simply could not allow it to continue. I turned onto Sixth Street and then took Division down to Green Street. As I pulled up to my mother's house, I noticed the front door wasn't open. Mama D always kept her door open when she was at home.

I parked the car and walked up to the front door. I turned the knob, but the door was locked, which was very odd. I fumbled for my keys, and after finally finding them, opened the door. The house was very quiet. I called for Mama D and got no response. After checking the living room and kitchen, I headed back towards Mama D's room, and the door was slightly ajar. Through the cracked door, I could see Mama D lying on the floor. I pushed the door open and ran to her. She didn't appear to be breathing. I screamed for Joy, but got no response.

125

Finally, I reached for my cell phone and dialed 911. I told the operator that I found my mother unconscious and to send an ambulance right away. The man on the phone was very nice; he told me to remain calm and said he would stay on the phone with me until the paramedics arrived. I held her hand, but it felt so lifeless. I started to cry as I thought about last night and how she didn't look good.

I shouldn't have left her alone, I thought to myself. *I knew she wasn't feeling well.*

I heard someone at the front door. I assumed it was the paramedics, but then I heard the scream from behind me. It was Joy. I let go of Mama's hand, stood up, and grabbed Joy to lead her out of the room. By now, she was yelling and sobbing.

"Oh my God, what's wrong with Mama D?"

"Calm down. I just arrived about five minutes ago and found her like this. I called for an ambulance, but I don't know what happened. Do you?"

She shook her head no, but didn't verbally say anything.

"Joy, where were you last night? Are you just coming home now?"

Through tears, she explained, "I went out with some of my friends from school. We went skating and then we all stayed over Lakisha's house for the night. Mama and I had a fight. She didn't want me to go because she doesn't like Lakisha, but I went anyway."

I grabbed her by the shoulders. "Listen, you and I will talk later about what happened last night, but for now, we need to both remain calm and tend to Mama D."

Joy nodded her head, acknowledging she understood. Just then, the paramedics arrived. I pushed Joy out of the way and met them at the front door. I showed them into Mama D's room, and they immediately started assessing her condition. They worked on Mama D for at least fifteen minutes before they got her prepped and ready for the trip to the hospital. I wanted to ride in the ambulance with Mama D, but I decided to drive so I could talk to Joy and try to calm her down. I called Toni, told her what was going on, and asked her to meet me at the hospital.

When we arrived at the hospital, we were taken to the emergency waiting room. Within minutes, Toni appeared with Lil' Darien.

As I stood up to take the baby from her, I asked, "Why did you bring him with you?"

"I didn't have time to find a sitter. I wanted to get here as soon as possible."

I could tell she was very concerned. I sat down next to her and told her everything that I knew, which was very little. When Joy went to the restroom, Toni asked how she was holding up. I explained how she came in while I was waiting for the paramedics but that I had gotten her calmed down.

The three of us sat in silence, taking turns holding and playing with Lil' Darien. Finally, about two hours later, a doctor appeared and walked towards me. He motioned for me to follow him into a private room. I turned to Toni and told her to give Lil' Darien to Joy so she could come with me. Joy protested a bit, but then agreed once I gave her a stern look. We followed the doctor into the private conference room. He closed the door and offered us a seat before he began speaking.

"Mr. Dickerson, your mother has suffered a massive stroke."

Toni and I gasped, and she grabbed my arm to pull me closer to her.

"Will she be okay?" I asked.

"Well, Mr. Dickerson, it was pretty serious, and the fact that she was alone for so long makes it hard to say. I will tell you that the next twenty-four hours will be critical. Since she is still unconscious, we really haven't been able to fully assess her condition."

Toni was sobbing uncontrollably. I was trying to hold it together, but tears were streaming down my cheeks, also.

"Doctor, can we see her?" I asked.

"We're getting ready to move her to a room in the ICU ward. Once she's there and stable, two visitors will be allowed in for fifteen minutes at a time."

"Thank you, Doctor."

"Okay, I will send a nurse to get you as soon as she is settled. Feel free to stay in this room as long as you like."

After the doctor left, Toni and I remained in the room holding and trying to console each other. We talked about how to break the news to Joy and decided to call her into the private room to tell her in case she broke down. Toni left to bring Joy and Lil' Darien into the room. Joy was already crying before I could explain everything the doctor told us. She felt responsible. Even though I did feel like some of this was her fault, now was not the time to discuss it. Instead, I hugged her and told her it wasn't her fault. Mama D had high blood pressure and was at risk of having a stroke.

We stayed in the conference room for about an hour talking to Joy and trying to get her calmed down. I decided Toni would go home with Lil' Darien after she'd had a chance to visit with Mama D briefly. Joy would stay with us until Mama D was stable and back home. Almost as soon as we got settled back in the waiting room, a nurse came looking for me. She looked very concerned.

"Mr. Dickerson, please come with me right away."

Without saying a word, I stood up and followed her as I could tell it was urgent. Toni and Joy stayed behind. The nurse led me down a hallway and into a small room similar to the room we were in previously.

Once there, she said, "The doctor will be right in to speak with you."

I sat down and tried to remain calm, but I had a very bad feeling about this. When my head started to throb, I put it down, closed my eyes, and started to pray. In the middle of my prayer, I heard the door open. I opened my eyes and saw the doctor standing in front of me.

He stood there for a moment before asking, "Mr. Dickerson, where is your wife?"

"Um, when the nurse called me back here, she stayed in the waiting room."

"Well, I'm going to go and get her before we talk."

He turned to leave, but I stopped him.

"Doctor, please just tell me what's going on. If it's bad news, just tell me."

He stopped with his hand still on the doorknob. He sighed heavily and turned back around to face me.

"Mr. Dickerson, did you know your mother had a DNR on file?"

Having no idea what he was talking about, I asked, "What is a DNR?"

He pulled a chair out from the table and sat down in front of me. "A DNR is a Do Not Resuscitate order, which means your mother didn't want us to go to any extreme measures to save her life."

I shifted in my seat and thought about what he had just said. He was talking in the past tense. After a minute, I said, "Doctor, are you saying my mother is dead?"

He cleared his throat and replied, "Yes, Mr. Dickerson. I am very sorry, but when we were moving your mother, she went into cardiac arrest and stopped breathing. Based on the DNR in her file, we didn't take extreme measures to save her life."

I couldn't believe what I was hearing. The room started to spin, and I felt like I was going to pass out. I could hear the doctor talking, but I couldn't make out what he was saying. He got up from the chair and left the room. As soon as he left, the nurse came in with a cup of water for me. I sat there staring at the cup and thinking about Mama D, and it felt like every memory I had of her was coming back to me. It was as if I was watching a movie of my life. I heard the door open again, and Toni ran towards me crying with her arms stretched out.

"Darien, babe, I'm so sorry. The doctor just told me what happened."

I was full of emotion, but I couldn't cry. It seemed as if I had shed all of the tears earlier and nothing would come out now. Toni held me until all of her tears were shed. We both knew Joy was going to have a terrible time dealing with the news. We talked and decided we would take Joy home before we broke the news to her.

After collecting myself, Toni and I went to the waiting room to get Joy and Lil' Darien. I asked Toni to take Joy by the house to get some things so she could stay with us. I took Lil' Darien and headed to our house.

During the drive home, I called Vince and gave him the news. He was in shock and offered to come over to the house, but I told him I just wanted to be alone tonight. He said he understood and would check on me tomorrow.

Toni

As I drove Joy over to Mama D's house, I felt very uncomfortable not telling her what had happened. Fortunately, she was very quiet and just sat looking out of the window the entire time. When we arrived at the house, she asked me to come inside with her, and I did. She quickly gathered her things, and we were on our way back to the house to meet up with Darien. When we arrived, Darien was just putting Lil' Darien to bed. Once I showed Joy to the guestroom, she said she wanted to take a shower and get ready for bed.

I found Darien sitting in the dark on our bed. As soon as I walked into the room, he said, "I cannot believe she's gone, Toni."

I rushed over and sat down beside him. Grabbing his hand, I told him, "I know, babe. It's a shock to me, too. Listen, Joy is in the shower right now. Are you going to talk to her tonight?"

Darien moved his hand from mine and hung his head down. "Toni, I have no idea what to say to her. I cannot help but feel like this is partly her fault."

"Darien, you can't tell her that. Even if it is true—and I'm not saying it is—but even if it were, you cannot tell her that. She was already struggling to find herself, and now she just lost her mother. She already feels responsible."

Darien turned to look at me. "I know all of that. I'm just telling you how I feel."

I stood up and said, "Okay, Darien, why don't we both talk to her once she gets out of the shower."

He looked at me and nodded his head in agreement.

Once Joy finished showering, we called her into the family room. Darien started the discussion, and I took over once Joy became upset. The three of us stayed up most of the night talking about Mama D, laughing, and crying. After Joy went to bed, Darien and I went to our room and talked some more. He was still very emotional and in shock about everything, but he switched into business mode. He talked about going to the house to look for her important papers. He was jumping way ahead, talking about what to do about the house and Joy.

I let him go for a little while before finally saying, "Let's get some sleep, babe. You're right; we have a lot of do and to think about, but right now, I want you to get some rest. Today was a very hectic day."

He responded by cuddling up close to me and giving me a kiss.

Then he said, "Toni, I love you and really don't know what I would do without you in my life."

I hugged him tighter and replied, "I love you, too, baby. Now let's get some rest."

I knew Darien was exhausted, because within five minutes, he was snoring. I was dead dog tired myself, but I couldn't sleep. I knew Lil' Darien would be up soon for a bottle, so I slowly slid out of the bed so I wouldn't wake Darien and headed downstairs. Right when I hit the bottom step, I heard a noise coming from the family room. For a brief moment, I forgot about Joy being in the house. When I entered the room, I found her sitting at the computer desk. Sensing my presence, she turned around.

"Hey, Toni. I couldn't sleep. I hope you don't mind me using your computer."

"No, Joy, it's okay. I couldn't sleep either. So how are you holding up?"

She sighed heavily. "It really doesn't seem real to me. I feel bad that she was alone. I know I should've been there with her, Toni. If I had been home like I was supposed to be last night, she would not have laid there so long alone."

She started to cry, and I went over to her to comfort her. As I held Joy and let her cry, I realized there were going to be some tough times ahead for Darien and I. Obviously, we were going to be responsible for Joy, and I had no experience at all dealing with a teenager. I really wish I could call Jada and talk to her, but I know she is still upset with me. I have known her a long time, and I knew that based on everything that went down, she was going to need a minute. I could really use my friend right now. I needed someone to talk to.

I felt guilty about the thoughts I had earlier this morning before I went to the hospital. After Darien left to go over to Mama D's house, I sat and re-read the letter from Benjamin several times. Even though I knew it was from over seven years ago, I felt something each time I read it. Last night when Darien asked me if I still loved Benjamin, I said no. I honestly wasn't sure what I felt right now. I fell asleep in the arms of my loving husband, yet my dreams were filled with thoughts of Benjamin. Right before Darien's phone call, I was in the process of writing an email to Benjamin to let him know I read the letter and how I felt about it. I felt like the timing of Darien's phone call was divine intervention, because deep within my soul I knew I couldn't let Benjamin know that I felt anything towards him any longer. If I opened up to him in any way, he would not stop until I was his again.

I smiled to myself at the thought of him fighting for me. As soon as I realized what I was doing, I shook my head to erase those memories. I had to stop being selfish, only thinking about my wants and needs. I needed to focus on my husband and my sister-in-law and the loss they just suffered. I needed Jada, my voice of reason, to talk me out of doing anything stupid, but calling her right now was not an option.

Chapter 15

Gina

I worked most of the night Saturday and all day Sunday on the article about David, Jr. I knew when I presented it to Susan today she would be very pleased. I had gone back and forth several times on the angle I wanted to take with this follow-up story. I finally decided to center it around the family memorial, without all of the extra drama of course. I wrote about the intimate family gathering I had attended. I wrote about some of the stories his friends and family recanted in his honor. I specifically highlighted David, Sr.'s story about how close they were and how proud he was of him and his accomplishments even though David, Jr. had not followed in his footsteps.

I was in my office putting the finishing touches on my article when my phone rang.

"Good morning. This is Gina."

"Good morning, Gina. This is Victoria."

Her voice sounded very different, not as timid as before.

"Hey, Victoria, how can I help you?"

"Well, I was just checking in with you to see how things were going with the story."

"Actually, I was planning on calling you today to discuss that with you. You see, there has been a new development, and I will not be running your story."

I heard a loud scream, and then she said, "What do you mean you're not running my story? You promised me. What new developments?"

"Listen, Victoria, I can't explain everything to you right now, but I will tell you that your story is no longer news because Jada and everyone else that was involved now know the truth."

"So you told them without printing my story? I can't believe you did this to me, Gina."

I was confused by her reaction. I thought the truth about Benjamin not being the one who attacked her was the purpose of her wanting her story told. I started getting a very different vibe from her now. She almost sounded desperate.

"Victoria, I didn't do anything to you," I replied to her accusation. "I know I said I would publish your story, but Jada found some letters that Benjamin wrote to Toni while he was in prison, and now everything is out in the open."

It sounded like she was throwing things around, and I could feel the tension through the phone.

"Gina, trust me, dear, everything is NOT out in the open. That story I gave you was just the tip of the iceberg, darling."

Not only did her statement confuse me, but I was also intrigued.

"Victoria, what are you—?"

Before I could finish my question, I heard the line go dead. I sat staring at my phone for a few minutes. I could not believe she flipped out about me not running the story and hung up on me. I wanted to call her back, but I didn't have time. I had to meet with Susan to go over the article. Miss Drama Queen Victoria was going to have to wait until later. I printed off my article, gathered my things, and headed down to Susan's office.

Victoria

I couldn't believe Gina was not going to run the story. Things were not going according to my plan at all. I needed that story to run in order to put the wheels in motion for my plan to ruin David, Sr. I was tired of him playing God and trying to control everyone's lives. My parents had allowed him to come in and dictate how things happened after the incident between David, Jr. and me. Only David and I knew the truth about what happened that night, and I was holding onto that for my final showdown with David, Sr.

I knew something was up when he called earlier this morning to make sure I had everything I needed. He never let on that Jada knew about David, Jr. and me, but what he doesn't know is that he's met his match with me. All this time he thought he was monitoring me, and all along, I've been watching him. He's still trying to control things, and I had the proof from his recent visit to Chicago. It was clear that Gina wasn't going to help with my plan, so I would have to take matters into my own hands.

David, Sr.

The first thing I did when I got to the office this morning was call and check on Victoria. She seemed surprised to hear from me, but said everything was good and that she didn't need anything. I considered letting her know that Jada had found out everything, but thought better of it. My next task was to contact Gina to get Samantha's information so I could have her added into my will. I also wanted to set up a time to go meet Samantha.

I checked my messages and had one from Benjamin, who said he was just checking on me to see how I was doing. He knew Saturday was tough for me. As I listened to his message, I shook my head. This man was loyal to a fault. *With everything that has come out in the open, does he not see that I set him up?* Sure, I cared for Benjamin, but he was not my son, and I was going to do whatever I needed to in order to protect my flesh and blood.

I sat in my office thinking about how being exposed to the media would be a disaster to my career. I was certain Gina was going to do a follow-up story since she mentioned it on Saturday, but I needed to know what she was going to reveal. I couldn't risk being disbarred. I looked her number up and dialed.

"Hello, this is Gina. How may I help you?"

"Hi, Gina. This is David, Sr."

"Oh, hi, David. It's so nice to hear from you. Are you feeling better? I know Saturday was rough for you."

I smiled at the thought that she cared how I was feeling.

"Yes, dear, but I'm doing well. Saturday was quite hectic and very unexpected. I really don't like surprises, which is why I'm calling."

"Okay. Well, how can I help you, sir?"

"Well, first, you can start by not calling me sir."

Gina chuckled. "Okay, David Sr., that's easy. What else can I do?"

"Well, I was wondering about the story you mentioned on Saturday. Are you still going to run the follow-up story on David, Jr.'s life?"

"Yes, sir...I mean, David, Sr. I'm going to run the follow-up story. In fact, I have been working on it all weekend."

I was very nervous about this and not sure how to broach the subject with her, but I decided to use the direct approach.

"So are you going to mention anything in your story about the incident in college?"

"Oh no, sir, I would never do that."

I breathed a sigh of relief as Gina continued.

"I mean, I have to be honest. I was going to initially, especially after I interviewed Victoria, but then I realized I would only be hurting Samantha and his other children. So, I rewrote the entire article. I just submitted it to my editor this morning for her to review."

Wait a minute. Did she say Victoria?

I switched the phone to my other ear and said, "You interviewed Victoria?"

Gina hesitated for a moment and then responded, "Um…yes, sir, I did, but I wasn't supposed to tell you or anyone else about that. Now that I've decided not to include her story, I guess it's okay that I mention it to you."

I was so angry I was shaking. I had just talked to Victoria, and she sounded as sweet and innocent as ever. All the while, she had gone behind my back and talked to Gina, a reporter. It was time for me to pay Victoria a visit. Talking over the phone was not going to cut it this time.

I decided to change the subject with Gina and talk about Samantha. I didn't want her to notice my change in mood.

"Gina, the reason I called was to get Samantha's date of birth and social security number. Oh, and also to discuss when I could meet my granddaughter."

I sensed Gina was smiling through the phone.

"Well, you can come to meet her whenever you want. I have to warn you that she looks just like David, Jr."

Now it was my turn to smile. My eyes started to water as I thought back to when David was a baby. It was still hard for me to think about him and not become emotional. It's just not natural for a parent to lose their child.

"Well, I would like to come up to see her sometime this week, if that's okay with you," I finally responded.

"Sure. I work during the day, and she stays at home with the nanny. But, let me know when you're coming, and I'll make sure we're both available."

"Thanks, Gina. I'm really looking forward to it. Let me check my schedule, and I'll be in touch."

I ended the call with Gina, sat back in my chair, and looked out of my office window over the harbor. I thought about Jada. I knew it was too soon for me to try to reach out to her. She would need more time. I quickly shifted my focus to Victoria and thought about how to handle her. I considered calling her parents, but she was an adult. Clearly, they had no influence on her in the first place or none of this would have happened. I picked up the phone and dialed my private investigator's number.

"Hi, Randy. So do you care to explain to me how Victoria was able to make contact with the reporter who interviewed my son?"

It seemed that I had caught him off guard because he did not respond.

"Don't worry about trying to answer me, Randy. I already know the answer. You slipped up. Therefore, what I need you to do now is retrace her steps to find out how she made the connection to Gina in Harrisburg all the way from Ohio. Do you think you can handle that?"

Finally, Randy spoke. "Um...yes, sir. I will get right on it and get back to you later today."

"Okay, Randy, and this is your last chance. If you mess up again, I'm going to have to find someone else I can trust to work with."

"Mr. Wright, that won't be necessary. I can handle this, I promise you."

I ended the call before he could give me any more excuses for his sloppy work.

Sitting in my office, I stared out over the harbor for a long time. I had dodged one bullet because Gina decided not to run the story about the incident in college. It was obvious to me now that I needed to follow up with Victoria and quick, because if Gina wouldn't run her story, I was certain she would try to find someone else who would. I always had a feeling that Victoria was going to be difficult to handle. I remember when she came out of her coma; she was less than happy with her parents for agreeing to the terms and the money. I will never forget the look in her eyes when she screamed at me that she would get me back one day. Remembering those words and the look in her eyes gave me a chill down my spine.

I shook my head to shake the feeling and turned around to my desk. After making some notes about things to handle this week, I started to look at my schedule to determine when I could make a trip to Ohio to pay Victoria a visit. Even though Randy said he would handle it, the more I thought about the situation, the more I realized I needed to take matters into my own hands and quick. I buzzed my assistant and asked her to come into my office. Lisa appeared almost instantly.

"How can I help you, sir?" she asked.

"I need you to book a trip for me to Ohio for the end of this week."

Taking notes, Lisa looked up and asked, "Would you like the same location and accommodations as before, sir?"

I smiled and responded, "Yes, Lisa. Thanks so much."

As she turned and quickly headed out, I thought about how much I appreciated her. She was pleasant and paid attention to detail. I trusted her. She never asked questions, just did exactly as I asked. Good help was hard to find. Many of my attorney friends had trouble finding and keeping good help. I made a note to do something special for Lisa.

Victoria

I was packing for my trip to Chicago. Just as I was about to head out the door, my cell phone rang. I looked at the caller ID and rolled my eyes. When I saw who was calling, I thought about rejecting the call, but decided to answer and get this conversation over with quickly.

"Yes, Randy, how can I help you?" I said, trying to sound overly enthusiastic on purpose.

"You can help me by keeping David off my back. What are you up to now anyway?"

I sighed heavily into the phone. "Listen, don't worry about David. Everything is under control."

I heard some movement like he was switching the phone and then he whispered, "No, everything is not under control. He wants to know about the connection with the reporter Gina. He found out about it somehow, and he wants to know how it happened without my knowledge."

I sucked my teeth and said, "Just stall him for a few days. Tell him you have to check a few things out. I'm on my way to

Chicago, and when I return, I will have something for you to tell him about how the connection was made."

When he didn't respond, I pulled my cell phone away from my ear to check to see if the call was still connected.

"Hello, are you still there?"

"Yes, I'm still here," he finally responded with a sigh. "Well, Lisa called me and said he's planning a trip to Ohio later this week. So, I guess it's a good thing you're going to Chicago. I imagine he's coming to pay you a visit."

"Thanks for the heads up, and I will make sure to extend my Chicago trip so I miss his visit."

After the call ended, I gathered up my things and headed out the door to the airport. On the drive there, I thought about how I ended up in this mess in the first place. Randy worked for David, Sr. and was supposed to keep an eye on me. I noticed him following me around town a few years ago. I figured he was working for David, Sr., so I approached him and made him an offer he could not refuse. He was not a bad looking guy, and I had extra cash from the money David, Sr. sent every month. Initially, I offered to pay him to share some of his other assignments with me. I knew David, Sr. was always digging up dirt on people and blackmailing them. So, I figured Randy could help me gather additional information to use in my plan to get revenge on David, Sr.

As the saying goes, you should keep your friends close and your enemies closer. Therefore, I started a relationship with Randy to keep him close and loyal. So far, it has paid off, because his information has kept me one step ahead of David, Sr. Also, I've been able to track down other victims of David's lies and deceit. I have no idea how Randy and Lisa are connected, but having her right by David's side has been a godsend, too.

I was looking forward to this trip, as it seemed I was getting much closer to finding the crucial piece of evidence I needed to bring David, Sr. down. Thanks to his hush money, I was able to devote all of my time and energy to finding out as much as I could about his illegal dealings. He thought he was going to sneak up on me by coming to Ohio unannounced. Meanwhile, I was going to be digging up his dirt in Chicago. I smiled at the thought and reached to turn up the volume of the radio so I could hear my favorite song, "Just Fine" by Mary J. Blige.

"Yep," I said aloud. "Everything is going to be just fine."

Chapter 16

Toni

Darien and I spent all day making arrangements for Mama D's funeral service. We arranged for the service to be held on Wednesday. Darien is holding up okay, but I'm very concerned about Joy. She stayed in her room all day yesterday and didn't want to eat. I finally forced her to eat some soup for dinner. Today, she stayed home from school and just lay around the house crying all day until one of her friends stopped over to visit. I'm pretty sure it's the girl she was out with on Saturday night. Joy mentioned she fought with Mama D about her because she didn't like her being friends with her since she was so much older. In addition, Mama D thought the girl was too fast because she had a steady boyfriend. I'm not sure what Mama D's concerns were, because from the limited interaction I had with her, she seemed like a nice young lady. I would keep an eye on their friendship, though, and try to get to know Lakisha better before passing judgment on her.

They took a walk down to the park. Before they left, they were sitting on the porch out front, and I overheard some of their conversation. It appears Joy has some anxiety about possibly having to change schools. I hadn't even thought about that until I heard her mention it to her friend. Looking at things from her

143

perspective, I understood how all of these changes could be scary for her.

I remembered how hard it was for me when I moved the summer before I started junior high school. I was so angry with my mother that I didn't speak to her for almost the entire summer. I had established relationships with my friends all through elementary school. All we talked about during the last half of the year was going to junior high school together. Then right after our sixth grade graduation ceremony, my mother told me that we were moving all the way across town, and I would be attending a different junior high school. I was not happy then, but looking back on it now, it turned out okay. I met Jada, and we quickly became best friends. Just thinking back to how we met and all the things we had been through over the years made me want to pick up the phone and call her. I had called her at least a half dozen times since Saturday night with no response.

When I mentioned my concerns about Joy to Darien, he snapped at me. So, I decided to leave it alone. I know it's normal for her to be upset and grieving, but my concern is around the fact that she feels responsible. She continues to say it's her fault because she fought with her mother, and that if she had been home, she could have gotten her mother help sooner.

I canceled a meeting I had today with my boss to discuss when I planned to return to work. I rescheduled the meeting for next week, but I've really already decided that I'm going to request a leave of absence. I'm enjoying my time at home with Lil' Darien and am not ready to give that up yet. Darien and I had discussed the possibility of me staying home full time, but I really didn't want to give up my career. Of course, that was before the baby came. Now that he's here, I'm enjoying motherhood and want to look for ways to generate some income from home.

I also knew things with Joy were not going to be easy and that there was a lot of work to do cleaning up Mama D's house and getting it ready to be sold or rented out. Darien had to work since he was the breadwinner. Once things settle down after the funeral service, I will try to sit Darien down and discuss my plans with him.

Darien

I'm physically exhausted and emotionally drained. There is so much to do in preparation for the funeral service. I'm so thankful for Toni. I really don't know what I would do without her right now. Vince has been supportive during this time, as well. I'm so glad he and I talked on Saturday to clear the air. It appears the timing of that was perfect, because I really need my friend now more than ever.

Toni is worried about Joy, and honestly, I am, too, but I'm hoping as more time passes, things will improve for her. I certainly have a rough road ahead of me. Taking over responsibility for my teenage sister is certainly not something I had planned. I knew Joy's father was not going to provide any assistance, and there wasn't really anyone else but me.

Vince and I talked about Mama D's house. I had some decisions to make about what to do with it. Too bad Toni and I just bought our house, because I would love to raise Lil' Darien in the house I grew up in. Vince thinks renting it out might be the best solution for now since I'm not ready to part with it. My only concern is finding someone I trust to take good care of it.

Toni is right; I'm thinking too much right now. I need to take a minute and let the shock of all of this wear off. Then I can focus on all of this stuff. I decided I was going to go to the gym for a workout. That's something I hadn't done in awhile, and it used to be a regular part of my weekly routine. A good workout would help relieve some stress and allow me to clear my mind.

I got up from the desk in my office and headed towards the bedroom to change. After I changed into my workout sweats and t-shirt, I went downstairs to find Toni. I found her in the family room playing with Lil' Darien.

"Hey, Toni, I'm going to head over to the gym for a workout."

She looked up and smiled. "Okay, babe. After I lay Lil' Darien down for a little nap, I'm going to make some dinner. Everything should be ready for you by the time you get back."

"That sounds good," I said, looking around the room. "Where's Joy?"

"Her friends came over to visit, and they decided to take a walk down to the park. You don't mind that I said she could go, do you?" Toni asked.

I shook my head no. "Of course I don't mind. I don't want her stuck in the house all the time."

Toni picked up Lil' Darien and his things and headed towards me. She gave me a kiss, and I kissed Lil' Darien before she headed upstairs to put him down for a nap. Then I grabbed my keys and headed out the door to the gym. I decided I would call Vince from the car to see if he could meet me at the gym. It would be like old times.

Vince

I was still in shock from hearing about Mama D's sudden death. My boy really needed me now. We talked for a long time on the phone, and he just called and asked me to meet him at the gym. I was glad to have my friend back. Right before Darien's call, I had been in the middle of composing an email to my friend Greg. I was trying to set up some studio work in Chicago so I could plan to spend some time there over the next several months. I put the final touches on my email, attached my updated resume, and hit send. Then I gathered my gym bag and headed out the door to meet Darien at the gym.

Gina

My conversation with Victoria from earlier this morning still had me a little unsettled. I decided to try to call her to find out why she was so upset about me not running her story. The truth was out. Everyone who needed to know about Benjamin's innocence knew, so what else did she want? I looked up her number and dialed. It rang four times, and just when I was about to hang up, she answered.

"Hello, this is Victoria."

"Hi, Victoria. This is Gina. I wanted to call you back so we can finish our discussion. We got disconnected earlier."

I knew she had intentionally hung up on me, but I was going to play along like I didn't realize that's what really happened.

"Oh yeah, Gina, what can I do for you?" she said, sounding very disgusted when she realized it was me.

"I was calling you back to explain in more detail why I'm not going to run your story."

"Look, Gina, it's okay," she interrupted. "I understand that Jada and everyone else knows the truth about Benjamin now."

"That's true, and I thought that's what you wanted."

"Yes, that's part of what I wanted, but not all of it."

Confused, I said, "I don't understand, Victoria. What else would you be accomplishing by me running that story besides hurting people like David, Sr.? And what about the negative impact it could have on David, Jr.'s children?"

"Gina, I'm on my way out of town, so I really don't have time to get into all of this with you right now. What I will tell you is that I really don't care one way or another about hurting David, Sr., and if you don't do anything else I tell you, please listen to me when I tell you to stay as far away from that man as possible."

The sound of disdain in her voice as she spoke about David, Sr. shook me to my core. I really didn't understand, but I decided to end this conversation since I felt I wouldn't get any answers from her.

"Okay, Victoria, I really don't understand all of this, but since you're short on time, I will let it go for now. If you want to continue this conversation, call me after your trip. In the meantime, I did email you a copy of the article I printed about David, Jr."

"Gina, stay away from David, Sr.," she warned, and then the line went dead.

Benjamin

I spent the entire weekend reflecting on everything I had learned about David, Jr. since I got out of prison. I was shocked at some of the things; he was my closest friend, and I could never imagine him doing those things. I remember the night I came into the room and found him beating Victoria. Initially, I was in such shock that I was unable to react. I had never seen that side of him. Even though I knew he was drunk, it just seemed to be a little extreme of a reaction to being accused of rape. Deep down inside, I always felt there was more to what happened that night between them than I was told.

Now I find out that he cheated on Jada during their marriage and had a child with another woman. None of this sounded like the David, Jr. that I knew and loved as a friend. I thought about David, Sr. and how hard it must have been on him to have everything he tried so hard to keep in the dark come to the light. He looked so helpless and out of control. I called him this morning to check on him, but had not heard back from him yet.

I continued to replay the events of Saturday night in my head, and the one thing that stuck with me was the image of hurt and pain in Jada's eyes. Jada had been hurt and deceived by almost everyone who was close to her—David, Jr., David, Sr., Toni, and me. However, Jada seemed to view me as a hero now that she understood what I did.

To think I lost the love of my life in order for my friend to have his family, and then he chose to disrespect their union by cheating. The thought of it made me angry, but also very sad for Jada and even Toni. I saw pain in her eyes, also. She's married and even possibly in love with Darien, but I know we still have a connection. I silently hoped that Derrick would be our child together. I know Toni, and I know that having a child together would solidify the bond that I knew was still there.

Victoria

My flight arrived in Chicago a little behind schedule. I was pleased that my contact was still waiting for me at the baggage claim area as expected. After I grabbed my bag, we headed to the car, and as we drove to the hotel, I was briefed on everything. I smiled while listening to all of the information about David, Sr. and his connections here. I was certain Randy would be very pleased once I got back and filled him in on my findings.

David had been pulling strings and changing peoples lives for years, and he had no idea that I was about to blow his entire operation wide open. David, Jr. knew how powerful his father had been, and he was ashamed of some of the things his father had done. He confided in me early on in our relationship about some of the things he was aware of that his father was involved in. David, Jr. had given me the ammunition I needed to get revenge on David, Sr.

No one, not even my own parents, knew the extent of my relationship with David, Jr. everyone assumed we met that fateful night. That was far from the truth. David and I met several years before that night. We met during one of the team's trips for a basketball game. I was an aspiring athletic trainer and frequently volunteered my time at the local college games to learn more about my intended field of study. David, Jr. wasn't a starter on the team, but he did play occasionally. We met and there was an instant attraction. I was still in high school, and he was supposedly in a serious relationship with Jada, but that didn't stop us from starting our own relationship. We would meet at least once a month to see each other unbeknownst to anyone, including Benjamin, his closest and dearest friend.

We fought that night because he told me about Jada being pregnant and their plans to marry. I threatened to go public about our relationship and to expose some of his father's hidden secrets from the past. I pushed him too far, and in his drunken state, he lost it and beat me into a coma. I knew what had happened, but even though I was hurting emotionally knowing that someone I loved had hurt me so bad, I could not bear the thought of David, Jr. going to jail for what he had done to me. My love for David, Jr. made it that much easier to go along with David, Sr.'s lies. The part I hated was the "no contact with anyone involved" stipulation. That meant no contact with David, Jr. I was confident that despite the stipulation David, Jr. would contact me. As I recovered, I patiently waited for him to reach out to me. After a full year of not hearing from him, I sought him out. The reunion was not what I expected. David was not happy to see me.

I showed up at his job one day. He was livid and told me there was no future for us. He kept reminding me about the deal and that I had agreed to take money from his father. Ultimately, I think that was what made him turn on me. He looked at me differently because of the money, even though I tried to explain to him that my parents agreed to the arrangement without my knowledge and my protest wouldn't have mattered anyway since I was a minor. In the end, none of it mattered. He was married to Jada, and they had their son. Nothing we had or talked about previously mattered to him anymore. I left Harrisburg that day feeling very hurt and alone. On my way back to Ohio, I vowed to get David, Sr. back for turning his son against me.

Over the years, I would contact David once a year like clockwork in hopes that over time, he would soften and be willing to continue a relationship with me. It never happened. When I heard about the accident and his death, I once again fell into a deep depression. I was completely out of it for nine months. Once I finally came back to reality, I decided enough was enough and that David, Sr. needed to be dealt with. I put my plan in motion to exact revenge on him.

This Chicago connection turned out to be a lot more involved than I first suspected, but I wasn't going to back down. What started as a way to get back at David, Sr. had turned into much more. I learned that David, Sr. had affected so many people's lives over the years, and the truth had to come out. It was going to take some time for me to go through everything and make sense of it. It was also clear that this was bigger than me. I was going to need some assistance with getting justice for everyone who David had wronged over the years. Although I missed David, Jr., I was glad he was not alive to witness his father's downfall.

Jada

Well, I did it. I found out the truth that no one wanted to tell me and then some. The intimate gathering to honor my deceased husband had ended with everything being out in the open. I knew about Benjamin going to jail for a crime that my deceased husband had committed. I knew about his affair with Gina and their love child, Samantha. I knew that my best friend, who I thought I could trust, kept both secrets from me.

I had spent the last week in bed crying and sleeping. My mother and father stayed and took care of the kids for me. My mother allowed me to keep to myself and process everything for three days before she attempted to discuss any of it with me. When she finally did try I wasn't ready. I tried to communicate how I felt and I couldn't put it into words, only tears. On the fifth day she did all of the talking. She told me how much she and my father loved me and that they both understood that I had experienced a horrible betrayal and it was natural to feel hurt and disappointed, but I had responsibilities to attend to, my kids and my job were both suffering. When she mentioned the kids I began to cry again. I had been so self-absorbed; I hadn't even considered the affect my breakdown was having on the children. It was then that I knew that something had to change in my life and quick.

That was three days ago. After that pep talk from my mother I snapped out of my depressed state and I was on a mission to get back on track. I knew that I had to leave the past behind me and move forward with my life for me and my children. After a day of seeing me up and about my parents felt comfortable enough to leave me alone. They offered to take the kids back to their house for the rest of the weekend to allow me some time to prepare to return to work.

As I dressed for church, I knew today was truly going to be the first day of a new life for me. I was thankful that it was

151

Sunday, because I needed to be with my church family today. I had somewhat abandoned them over the past year since David, Jr. died. I would attend services on Sunday, but I was literally just there physically. I wasn't really receiving the spiritual food being offered. I wasn't participating in any of the church activities like I had in the past. After last week, I knew I needed to refocus and reevaluate my life and my priorities. I had also decided that after church today, I would visit the cemetery to have another conversation with my late husband.

I arrived at church on time and took my seat right in the middle of the room, just as I did every Sunday. The preacher was on fire today. It felt like he was talking directly to me. The message was about forgiveness. I thought to myself, *Can I really forgive David, Jr. for causing all this pain I feel in my heart right now?* I also wondered if I would ever be able to face David, Sr., who was a major contributor to all of the secrets being kept and the lies being told.

After service was over, I headed out the door, and in my haste, I bumped into a man.

"Excuse me, sir. I'm so sorry. I wasn't paying attention to where I was going."

He looked somewhat familiar, but I just assumed I knew him from church.

"Oh, it's okay. I understand," he responded. "The preacher's message was a powerful one today. I was somewhat lost in my own thoughts, also, and wasn't really paying attention to where I was going. Hey, you're Toni's friend, right?"

I was taken aback by his reference to Toni because that meant I knew him from somewhere else, not church.

"Yes, I'm Toni's friend Jada. Do I know you?"

He laughed. "Well, you should since you were at my wedding."

As soon as he said that, I remembered who he was.

"Oh, yes, I remember you now. You're Darien's friend Vince. You're married to the reporter Gina, right?"

He looked very uncomfortable when I mentioned Gina's name and didn't respond right away.

"Sorry to pry. I didn't mean to make you uncomfortable."

He sighed heavily and said, "Gina and I are no longer together. We're in the process of getting divorced."

I tried my best to seem surprised and concerned, but I knew what the reason was behind all of this.

"Oh, I'm very sorry to hear that."

"It's okay. These things happen, and some things are just not meant to be. So how long have you been coming here?"

"I've been attending this church for about eight years now. This is the church my husband and I chose when we moved here."

"Wow. I've been coming here for as long as I can remember, and I don't ever remember seeing you here before."

"You know how small Harrisburg is, so we were going to run into each other one day eventually, right? Well, Vince, it was nice seeing you again, but I have to go. Maybe I will see you again next Sunday."

"Yes, I'm sure you will."

As I walked to my car, I thought about the coincidence of me seeing Vince this morning after finding out just last week that his wife was having an affair with my husband. Based on our conversation, I was certain he had no idea about Gina and David.

As I drove, I thought about what conversation I would have with David. When I first woke up this morning and decided I wanted to visit David's gravesite, I had an idea in my head of what I would say. However, after hearing the preacher talk about forgiveness, I felt the need to revise my speech. After arriving at his gravesite, I sat in the car to pray and collect my thoughts. Then I got out and headed towards his grave. Once there, I knelt down, said a prayer, and began talking to my husband.

During my talk with David, I cried, laughed, and cursed, even though I tried hard to keep my composure. When I walked away from his grave this time, I felt a sense of peace. Even though he had done some horrible things, I still loved him, and he had given me my beautiful children. He was dead, and his deeds were in the past. *I hope there is no one else who is still being hurt by his actions,* I thought as I got into my car and drove to pick up Tre and

Jordan from my parents' house. I desperately needed to hug my babies today.

Chapter 17

One month later
Vince

I was on my way to pick up my parents and head to the airport. I barely slept a wink last night; I was too nervous about the custody hearing tomorrow. It was hard to believe a month had passed already. My parents were excited and nervous, as well. In the past few weeks, my mother has called me more than she has in the past three years. Even though I tried to prepare her in case I didn't win the case, she insisted on setting up a room at her house for Derrick. She spent all of her time prepping the room. She painted it, sewed handmade curtains, and made it very kid friendly. My father was happy because it gave her something to focus on besides him.

I have continued to attend church regularly and have run into Jada a few more times. She seemed like a nice woman, and I was interested in getting to know her better. She seemed a little uncomfortable whenever the subject of her getting involved in a relationship was broached, so I decided to back off a bit for now. We had talked a few times about Derrick and the custody battle. She tried to encourage me and agreed that Derrick and Tre could meet and spend time together once I brought Derrick to Harrisburg.

Things seemed to be moving in the right direction. I had contacted Greg, and he has some studio work that could keep me busy for the next six months. My mother had been helping, too. She'd been searching the internet during the week trying to locate a place for me to stay in Chicago. She had narrowed my choices down to two places, and she and I had made a day trip out there a week ago to see both places and to make the final decision. If things worked out, I would be moving to Chicago for the next six months. I was being optimistic I knew, but in addition to packing for a week's stay, I also had the rest of my things packed up and ready for shipping. The plan was if I won custody, we would all stay for the first few days. Then my father would head back to Harrisburg to ship the rest of my things.

We were traveling a day early to ensure there were no flight delays. Making this court date was the most important thing right now. My lawyer seemed to think things were in my favor. The divorce between Derrick's adoptive parents was still not final, and things didn't seem to be getting any closer to being final. They were hurting their chances for gaining custody of Derrick with all of the bickering. All of this was in my favor, and I was hopeful the judge would see what was in the best interest for Derrick.

Toni

Journal Entry

So much time has passed since I have written. It has been almost a month since Mama D passed, and Darien and I are adjusting to our new life as the parents of a teenager. Joy has adjusted nicely to the move to our house. Initially, it was very difficult for her to go to her house and pack up her things. Darien has met with her principal and the counselor at school, and they arranged for Joy to remain in her current school instead of transferring her in the middle of the year. Everyone agreed that with everything else she had been through, making a drastic change of schools right now would not be good for her. Joy was ecstatic when Darien announced she didn't have to change schools. He did give her some expectations, such as she had to maintain at least a B average in all of her classes. He also told her that she would have to participate in at least one after school activity. Joy agreed to his conditions, and so far, things were going well.

I suggested counseling sessions, as well, and surprisingly, Joy agreed. She seemed to be enjoying her weekly sessions, and I was very pleased because her counselor encouraged her to journal about her feelings. Journaling was my thing, too. So, after dinner most nights, Joy and I met in the family room, and we each curled up on our respective chairs with our journals to write.

I have taken a leave of absence and have taken over the task of cleaning up and preparing Mama D's house for rental. In addition to that, I'm researching stay-at-home jobs and have a few viable options I am considering. Darien went back to work after only one week and seems to be handling things as well as can be expected. He's handling all of the probate and estate stuff with the state. Lil' Darien is growing like a weed and I am enjoying my additional time at home with him. Having Joy around is also helpful for me with the baby. Things are really coming together, all except for my friendship with Jada.

It's been a month, and she still isn't returning my calls. I have called, texted, emailed, and even sent her a card in the mail. She hasn't responded to any of it. I have driven past her house a few times, but decided against ringing the doorbell once I got there. I have known Jada a long time, and I knew that eventually she would respond once she was ready.

It was as if a part of my life was missing. Jada was a link to all of the memories of Benjamin and me and the love we shared. I have been so busy I haven't had a chance to think about Benjamin or allow the feelings that came rushing back once I read his letter to affect me. Deep down, I knew if Jada and I were talking right now, it would be much harder to ignore those feelings and move on with my life.

Gina finished her follow-up story on David, Jr., and it turned out to be a nice article. Strangely enough, she and I have kept in touch over the past few weeks. Seems like she needed someone to talk to, and since our babies are so close in age, we had that in common. I found her to be nice, even though Darien questioned me about forming a friendship with her. He thought it was odd for me to be friends with the woman who slept with my best friend's husband. I would agree with him if David were still alive or if Jada was talking to me. I didn't have many other friends in Harrisburg, so spending time with Gina and talking to her on the phone was good for me. Since moving here, I spent most of my time working or with the string of men who had all been a waste of my time. I needed a friend to spend time with, and right now, Gina seemed to be exactly what I needed.

Jada

I have avoided everyone since the memorial for David. The most persistent person had been Toni. She called, texted, and emailed me constantly, but I wasn't ready to deal with her right now. I did feel bad because I had heard about Darien's mother passing away. Still, I needed some time just for me.

I've spent my free time cleaning out my house, finally removing all traces of David except for a few pictures. I cleared out his office and made it a playroom for the children. I reconnected with people at church. I also have begun to participate in more church activities, such as bible study, and I put the kids back in the children's choir.

I have run into Vince a few more times at church, and he even sat next to me one time. We've chatted a few times after service, and he filled me in on his custody battle for Derrick. We discussed having Tre and Derrick meet once he came to Harrisburg so Derrick would have someone his own age here to play with.

Vince seemed like a nice person. I sensed he might be interested in getting to know me better, but I'm really not ready for anything like that. David had been my first and only. I had no idea how to go about dating or getting involved with anyone else. My mother called me at least once a week suggesting that I join the singles ministry at the church. She thought the best remedy for a broken heart is to jump back into the game. Not only had my heart been broken, my entire world had been shattered. Losing the love of your life and then finding out they were not the person you thought they were is tough. What's worse is when they aren't around so you can get angry and ask them why they did what they did to you. You're left with unanswered questions and speculations for the rest of your life. Even though I had recently found out that it was all a lie, I still found it hard to believe my relationship with David, Jr. was not as special as I felt it was all these years.

The thought of opening up myself to someone else and trying to trust them seemed so far off for me. I did miss the companionship, though. Many nights after the kids were in bed asleep, I sat in my room looking around, wondering if I would ever find someone to connect with to fill the void. Obviously, David had a secret life outside of our life, but what we had together was good. There was a deep connection that I felt even now, and he's been gone over a year. I kept telling myself that when I was ready, God would put someone in my life.

The hardest part was trying to explain to the kids why David, Sr. had not been around. Tre asked for him often and sometimes wanted to call him, and I had to come up with excuses. Next to Toni, David, Sr. was the next in line for the number of attempts to talk to me. He has left several messages begging me to call him and telling me how sorry he was and that he missed the children.

The story that Gina ran about David's life was wonderful. She did an excellent job of portraying him as the man he was to everyone else. To the outside world, he was this wonderful, kind, and giving person whose passion was helping children to find their niche. No one needed to know that his personal life was a wreck or one big lie. I felt so proud of the story she had written that I cut it out and put it in the children's scrapbook that I started for them about their father. Once I read the story, I sent her a note asking her not to contact me again. She seemed like a nice enough person, but I could not get over the fact that she not only slept with my husband, but also had a child with him. Maybe one day when the pain isn't as fresh I can get past it. Our children should know each other, but how would I explain it to them? It was just too much to consider right now.

Benjamin was still and would always be my hero. I hadn't spoken to him since that night, but I received emails, cards, and an occasional text message from him. His message was always brief. It simply said, *Just checking in on an old friend.* After reading those letters, I now understood why Toni waited for him like she did for so long. She knew the kind of person he was, and she knew there was no way he would simply vanish from her life like that. I shook my head upon realizing I had that same kind of conviction about my relationship with David. I just knew we were each other's one and only, but boy, was I wrong.

I was a little jealous that Toni had been right about Benjamin. So many nights she cried about him and said she knew he would never abandon her. The thought of my husband and father-in-law being the reason they were not together now brought me to tears. The only thing that made it bearable was the fact that she had found love again with Darien. I was actually inspired by that. I figured if Toni could find true love twice in her lifetime, then there was hope for me, as well.

I really did miss Toni and our friendship. The kids even asked about her from time to time, and I realized I was missing valuable time with my godson. I was still hurt and angry, but I thought I might reach out to her and ask if she would bring the baby over so I could see him. I decided I would respond to her latest email and suggest we get together for lunch to talk and spend time with the kids.

I went over to my desk and pulled up her last email from just a few days ago.

Jada,

> *Please talk to me. I miss you and need you.*

Toni

I smiled while reading it because I felt the exact same way. I decided to respond with something I knew would make her smile, as well.

Toni,

You had me at hello. Let's meet for lunch tomorrow at noon. Come here to the house and bring my godson, or I won't let you in.
Jada

Victoria

I had gathered some very useful information during my trip to Chicago last month. I spent the past month tracking down more information and trying to confirm that the sources of my information were accurate and credible. I considered going to visit David, Sr. and telling him about the information I had gathered about all of the cases where he paid witnesses to disappear. After digging into all of the information I had compiled, I decided against confronting him directly.

While digging through his old dirt, I found the reporter who was initially following the story about Benjamin being drafted into the NBA and who had vanished into thin air right around the time Benjamin reportedly experienced his career-ending injury. What I discovered is that David, Sr. was able to get away with these things because he was keeping secrets and doing favors for some influential people. I thought Gina would be the one to help me expose David and his deeds. This could have been the story that catapulted her career to a new level, but she failed her test. She broke her promise to print my story, so I had to move on.

Once I found Rhonda, the initial reporter, she and I decided to join forces to take David, Sr. down. With her connections, we were going to be able to make sure all the major networks ran the story. His unscrupulous tactics to win cases being aired on all major networks would certainly come as a complete shock to him. He wouldn't have a chance to pay anyone off to kill the story.

The information we gathered had to be verified before any of the stations would run the story. We were confident we could get national coverage of the story because of the fact that some of the people involved were in the sports and entertainment industry. I did feel bad about exposing their dirt, but when I started investigating David, Sr., I had no idea just how deep his scheming had gone over the years.

Toni

I put Lil' Darien down for a nap and decided to catch up on my emails. I had sent another one to Jada a few days ago and checked to see if she had finally decided to respond to me. Upon opening my email account, I couldn't believe my eyes. Not only had she responded, but she also invited me to her house for lunch. I closed my eyes and said a silent thank you to God. I had been praying that He would bring my friend around.

Chapter 18

Vince

The custody hearing was brief. I don't know what I was expecting, but once everyone was there, the judge simply read his decision, which was I had been awarded full custody of Derrick. Derrick's adoptive mother silently wept once the judge announced his decision. The one condition, which my lawyer had prepared me for, was that Derrick remain in his current school, and there would be a transition period of approximately six months to allow him time to get to know me and to adjust. He would have regular visitation with his adoptive parents separately once a week as long as they wanted to remain in his life. I was granted permission to take Derrick out of state once a month.

I was very pleased with this outcome, as were my parents. I was very anxious to meet Derrick and get started making a life for us both. While we were leaving the courtroom, I decided to stop to talk with Derrick's adoptive mother. As I approached her, she wiped her eyes. When she looked up at me, I was struck by the beauty of her eyes. She had long brown hair that went halfway down her back. Her skin was a caramel complexion. It was her eyes that really caught my attention, though. They were light brown and full of sadness. Her eyes told the story of just how stressful the past few years had been.

Extending my hand to her, I said, "Hi, I'm Vince. Sorry to meet under these circumstances."

She took my hand and stood up. Once she stood, I was further in awe of this woman's beauty. She appeared to be approximately 5'7" and was a medium build, not too skinny and not too big, just right with curves in all the right places. Her poise and grace took me by surprise.

"Hi, Vince. I'm Martha. It's nice to meet you, too. I'm very concerned about Derrick. He has been through so much already. I just don't know if he can handle another major change in his life."

She sniffled and reached into her purse for another tissue. My instincts were telling me to grab her and give her a hug. I looked over my shoulder back to my parents and my lawyer, who was very agitated that I was talking to her. I decided against the hug, but I did reach into my pocket and pull one of my business cards out of my wallet to give to her.

I extended my card towards her and said, "Listen, Martha, I can only imagine how difficult this must be for you. I think it would be best if you and I work together to ensure that Derrick transitions well into his new life. Call me sometime if you would like to discuss how we could do that. I have an apartment and a job here for the next six months. I would love to talk to you about Derrick so you can fill me in more on his background."

She smiled, and once again, her beauty struck me.

"Yes, I would love to talk to you more about Derrick, and I do intend to make use of the weekly visitation with Derrick."

She took my card and put it in her purse. Then she extended her hand again to shake mine before turning to walk away. I watched her until she was completely out of my view. My father was the first to speak when I returned to them.

"Well, son, it seems like you made a friend and a cute one at that," he said, chuckling.

Before I could respond, my mother chimed in, "So when do we get to meet Derrick? I can't wait to meet my grandson."

My attorney answered for me. "Tomorrow, Derrick will be brought to the Children and Youth Services office by his foster parents. Vince, you will meet them there to pick him up and take him home with you."

"Can we go, too?" my mother asked.

"No, Mrs. Smith," Joe, my attorney, responded. "It's probably best if Vince comes alone. We don't want to bombard Derrick with too much and too many people at one time. I think it's probably best if you and Mr. Smith wait for Vince and Derrick at home. You could even decorate and have a little party planned for him or something to welcome him to his new home."

At first, my mother looked disappointed, but her eyes brightened when he mentioned having a welcome home party.

After we all agreed that would be the best approach, Joe excused himself and said he would meet me tomorrow at noon. My parents and I headed out to the car to return to my new apartment. We spent the remainder of the day getting the apartment ready for Derrick. I was so thankful for my parents being here to support me through this. I was very happy I had won the case, but also very nervous about what lie ahead for me. Let's face it. I had never been anyone's father before. I had very little to no experience with children at all. I knew Derrick might be somewhat of a handful because of all he has been through over the past few years. Thankfully, my mother was going to stay in Chicago with me for the first few weeks to help with Derrick while I got accustomed to having a son and my new job. My father planned to head back by the end of the week as long as things were going well.

I realized I should probably let Toni and Darien know the outcome of the custody case. So, I decided to text Darien, and then he could decide how he wanted to handle letting Toni know. I sent him a brief text that read, *I won. Picking him up tomorrow afternoon. I will send a picture. Please let Toni know.* Almost immediately, I received a response from Darien, which read, *Congrats, man! I am so happy for you.*

Smiling, I placed my cell phone down and lie back on the bed. I thought about my life and was amazed by how much things had changed over the past year. It goes to show you that even though we might have a plan, sometimes what God has planned for us is very different. I drifted off to sleep thinking about all of the challenges that lie ahead of me, and I kept thinking about Martha. I felt bad that she was losing the son who she had raised for the past eight years. I wondered about Derrick's adoptive father. He never appeared at any of the hearings; it was only Martha.

Morning came before I knew it, and Mom made a nice big breakfast. After breakfast, we finished preparing Derrick's room for his arrival. While dressing before heading to meet Joe at the Children and Youth office, I became very nervous. I parked and headed towards the entrance, where I saw Joe standing outside near the door waiting for me. He did not look very happy. As I approached and he saw me, he started shaking his head. My heart skipped a beat.

I hastened my pace, and once I was within earshot, I asked, "What's wrong, Joe?"

Shaking his head, he said, "Martha is here. She's demanding to see Derrick before you take him."

I breathed a sigh of relief. "Oh man, is that all?"

"Yes, but it's not good that she's here. You don't want her to see Derrick right before you take him to live with you, do you?"

I thought for a minute before replying, "Yes. Actually, I would like for him to see her before I take him. In fact, I would like for the three of us to talk—me, Derrick, and Martha."

Joe shook his head. "No, Vince, I really don't think that's a good idea."

People were walking past us, so I pulled Joe over to the side and said, "Why not? She is his mother. The only mother he has ever known prior to being placed in foster care a few months ago. Why shouldn't she be allowed to see her son and he be allowed to see his mother?"

Joe didn't respond right away. He looked around and seemed to be deep in thought.

Finally, he said, "Okay, it's your call, Vince. If you want to allow her to see him, I will let her attorney know."

Joe turned towards the building, then stopped and motioned for me to follow him. We took the elevator to the third floor, and once we got off the elevator, I saw her immediately. When she saw me, a slight smile came over her face, but it immediately faded when she looked at Joe. I recognized her attorney from the court proceedings present, as well. Joe approached her attorney; they spoke in whispers; and then her attorney leaned over to whisper in her ear. As he spoke, her demeanor changed and a bright smile came over her face. She turned towards me and mouthed, *Thank you.* I responded with an audible, "You're welcome."

Joe returned to my side and explained I would be taken into a room where the foster parents would bring Derrick. Initially, it would have been Derrick, the counselor, and me in the room. The counselor that Derrick and I have both been seeing individually had been preparing him for this day. He knew his birth father had located him and was seeking custody of him. Once Derrick and I met and had some time to spend alone with the counselor, Martha would be allowed to come in and see Derrick. Then the three of us could discuss what was happening. Joe explained it would be up to me to decide if I wanted the counselor to remain during Martha's visit.

As Joe talked, I looked over his shoulder at Martha, who was sitting in the hallway with her attorney. I had mixed emotions now about allowing her to see Derrick, but I couldn't change my mind now. I told Joe that I would decide when it was time. I needed more time to think. Before long, I was being taken to the room to await Derrick's arrival. Joe wouldn't be in the room with me.

I entered the room and started pacing back and forth. When I heard the door open, I turned to see the counselor, who I had a few sessions with during the custody battle. She had a file with her, which she placed on the table. Then she walked over towards me.

"Hello, Vince. How are you feeling today?"

I swallowed hard; my mouth felt very dry. "I'm doing well," I replied. "Just a little nervous about finally meeting my son."

Belinda smiled and nodded her head, letting me know she

understood.

"Well, that is normal and very understandable. I want to talk to you for a few minutes before Derrick arrives, so let's take a seat."

I moved towards the table and said, "Okay."

Belinda opened up her file, flipped through a few pages, and then began to explain to me what would happen when Derrick arrived. She would introduce us. Derrick knew I was his biological father, and she had explained to him what that meant. Belinda suggested I follow his cues. She explained that sometimes the children are overcome with emotion and want to hug you, while others are very scared and standoffish. She cautioned me not to become too emotional, if possible. As she explained everything to me, I found myself wishing my parents had been able to come with me. I felt very uncomfortable doing this alone.

As I thought about Martha sitting outside the room, I looked up at Belinda and asked, "Would it be okay if Martha comes in the room with me when they bring Derrick in to meet me?"

Belinda was taken aback by my question, but I could tell she liked the idea of it.

"Why would you want to do that?"

I stood and started pacing the room again. "I just feel like it would be better for Derrick to see us both at the same time. I think it could make the transition better if he saw Martha and I as a team and not as enemies on opposite sides fighting for him."

Belinda sat back and crossed her arms. "Vince, you are an amazing man." She closed her file, stood up, and said, "That is an excellent idea and approach. Let me notify Martha, and I will have her come in here now before Derrick arrives."

As Belinda left, I turned towards the window. I lowered my head and said a silent prayer for God to give me the strength to make it through this day. As soon as I finished my private conversation with God, the door opened, and I turned to see Martha standing at the door. She started walking towards me, and when we met, she held both of her hands out. I nervously extended my hands, and she grabbed them.

"Thank you so much for allowing me to be here today. We're both in this terrible situation, but what's most important is what is best for Derrick. He is a really good kid and doesn't deserve to have all of this drama in his life."

Before I could respond, the door opened again. Martha dropped my hands and turned towards Belinda, who walked in and announced they were bringing Derrick in now. Almost instinctively, Martha came and stood right beside me so that when Derrick entered the room, he would see us both standing side by side.

There was a light knock on the door, and Belinda opened it. There stood Derrick next to his foster mother. She gave him a slight nudge, and he walked into the room. He saw Belinda first, and then he looked past her to see Martha and me. When he looked at Martha, his eyes lit up. He slowly walked towards her while looking back towards Belinda to confirm it was okay. When Belinda gave him a slight nod, his pace increased, and when he reached her, he jumped into Martha's arms. As he hugged Martha, he kept both of his eyes on me. I tried to control my emotions, but a single tear escaped and rolled down my cheek.

Noticing it, Derrick pulled away from Martha and asked, "Mommy, why is the man crying?"

Martha turned towards me as she put Derrick down. "Derrick, that man is your father, and he's crying because he is happy to finally meet you."

Derrick's eyes widened. He walked towards me and extended his hand. I looked down at his face and then took his hand.

While shaking my hand, he said, "Hi, Dad. It's nice to finally meet you."

By now, tears were flowing freely down my cheeks. I looked up at Belinda because I knew she had advised me to remain calm and to follow his lead. She nodded that I was okay.

I knelt down before Derrick and said, "It's so nice to finally meet you, too, son. May I give you a hug?"

Derrick didn't respond. Instead, he simply opened his arms and gave me a hug.

Belinda came over to us and suggested we sit down and talk for a few minutes about what was going to happen. Derrick took Martha's hand and mine, and led us over to the table. Once we were all seated at the table, Belinda started to explain that Derrick would live with me. Belinda explained that my house was close to his school and in the same neighborhood. She also said he would be able to visit with Martha once a week. Derrick seemed to be okay with everything Belinda was telling him. Once she finished, she asked him if he had any questions. Derrick looked at Martha before he spoke and squirmed a little in his seat.

Finally, he looked at Belinda and asked, "Do I have to see Chuck every week, too?"

Martha immediately dropped her head, and I could tell she was uncomfortable with his question. I knew who Chuck was from the court papers. He was Martha's husband whom she was still trying to divorce.

Belinda responded, "No, honey. At this time, Chuck does not have any visitation rights."

Derrick seemed to relax a bit and sat back in his chair. Belinda looked at Martha first and asked if she had any questions. She said no. Then it was my turn. I asked if Martha could have more than once a week visitation with Derrick. When I asked the question, Martha turned to me, and I could see tears welling up in her eyes. She looked from me to Belinda, awaiting her response.

"The court will be monitoring the visits, which are weekly here at this office," Belinda finally answered. "In addition, Derrick must continue his weekly counseling sessions. Other than that, Mr. Smith, you can allow Derrick to see whoever you would like for him to see."

I smiled at Derrick and Martha. "That's great. I don't have any more questions."

As Belinda stood up and started gathering her things, she said, "Mr. Smith, you can leave with Derrick whenever you are ready. I have another case, so I need to get going." Then she looked at Derrick and said, "Derrick, I will see you next week during our scheduled session, okay?"

Derrick nodded in agreement.

There was an awkward silence for a few moments after Belinda left. Finally, Martha and my eyes met, and without communicating verbally, we both knew what was next. We stood up and headed out the door with Derrick in between us holding both of our hands. Once outside, Martha told Derrick that he was going to ride in the car with me, but she would follow behind us. Derrick seemed very comfortable with me, so he did not mind at all.

Toni

I had no idea why I was so nervous as I drove towards Jada's house. When I arrived, I pulled into the driveway. Immediately, the front door flew open, and Tre and Jordan came running out to my car. I opened my door and they leapt on me, not even giving me a chance to get out of the car.

"Auntie T, we missed you," they both said in unison. "Where have you been?"

I was caught off guard by their question, as I had no idea what Jada may have told them.

"Let's get the baby in the house and we can talk about that, okay?" I responded.

"Okay, Auntie T. Can we help you with the baby?" Jordan asked, smiling.

"Yes, you can carry the bag in for me, okay?"

She squealed with delight as I reached over the seat to grab the bag to hand it to her. She took it and sprinted towards the house. Tre had opened the back door and was playing with Lil' Darien.

"Excuse me, Tre. Let me get Lil' Darien out and into the house. Then you can play with him as much as you want."

He stepped back and said, "Okay, Auntie T."

After removing Lil' Darien and his car seat from the car, I nervously walked towards the door. I could see Jada standing in the doorway.

Once I reached her, she looked from me to Lil' Darien and said, "Oh my goodness! Look at how big he has gotten. Give me my godson, girl."

I smiled and handed the baby over. Our reunion was bittersweet.

Jada had prepared a nice lunch. After we got the kids settled, we went into the kitchen to talk.

"Jada, I am so sorry."

She interrupted me and said, "Toni, let's not go there." She paused briefly and then continued, obviously trying to change the subject. "So tell me, how are Darien and Joy doing?"

I was a little caught off guard by the change in direction of our conversion, but I decided to roll with it.

"They are both doing well," I responded. "Joy had a hard time initially, but she's going to counseling now, and it really does seem to be helping her."

Jada picked at her food, but wasn't really eating it.

"That's great. And how are you adjusting to being a full-time mommy for an infant and a teenager?"

This made me chuckle. "Things are good. It's a big adjustment. The decision to stay home was a tough one for me. You know how hard I worked to build my clientele and become one of the top marketing reps in our division."

Jada smiled. "Yes, girl, I do know. I was there every step of the way. Things are not the same without you around the office."

This made me smile. I took a sip of my tea and then asked, "So, Jada, how are you doing?"

She put her cup down and leaned back in her chair.

She smiled and responded, "You know what, Toni? I'm doing well. I had a rough few weeks at first, but I have finally turned the corner. I have gotten back involved in some activities at church and have gotten the kids involved, as well. Work is keeping me busy since I had to recruit for a replacement to handle your region."

She shot me an angry look and then rolled her eyes, which made me bust out laughing. Then there was a long pause; it seemed as if neither of us knew what to say next. Finally, I decided to say what I was thinking.

"Jada, I am very sorry for keeping everything from you, but I was trying to protect you. You had just experienced the worse kind of loss, and I really didn't think you needed to hear about all of this other stuff."

The entire time I was talking, Jada just stared at me with an emotionless expression.

Finally, she responded, "Toni, I understand that you didn't mean any harm, but please try to understand that everything I thought I knew about my husband and our life together was a lie. Everyone I trusted and loved betrayed me in one way or another."

As she spoke, tears started to form in my eyes and eventually made their way down my cheeks. I knew she was right. I had thought about all of those things myself, but to hear her say them was so painful for me.

"Toni," she continued, "I'm still hurting, and although I forgive you, I am still going to need some more time to come to terms with all of this."

I nodded my head to acknowledge that I understood.

"The kids really missed you, and I missed Lil' Darien. So, I wanted us to get together to get some things off our chest and to call a truce, but I'm in no way ready to just pick up where we left off."

Her last comment stung a bit, but I nodded in agreement and wiped a tear from my cheek.

"Jada, I understand, and we can do whatever you feel we need to in order for you to trust and be comfortable with me and our friendship again."

Just then, my cell phone rang. I looked at the caller ID; it was Gina. *Damn,* I thought to myself. I forgot I was supposed to meet her at the mall today for lunch. When I received Jada's email, I completely forgot about what I already had on my schedule.

"Jada, I need to take this call real quick."

She nodded and got up to go check on the kids.

"Hey, Gina," I answered. "I am so sorry, girl. I forgot to call you to let you know I had a conflict today. Can I call you back later?"

"Sure, Toni, no problem," Gina responded. "I will talk to you later."

As soon as I put my cell phone down on the table, I noticed Jada standing right in front of me with her hands on her hips. It never occurred to me until just now that she might overhear my conversation and actually have an issue with my talking to Gina.

Before I could start to explain, she said, "Toni, did you just say Gina's name?"

"Uh, yes, that was Gina," I replied tentatively.

"Okay, please explain to me why you would be talking to Gina?"

I could tell she was a little more than angry, so I decided to make my way towards the other room to gather up Lil' Darien and his things.

"Listen, Gina and I have been hanging out a little bit for the past few weeks. Our kids are around the same age, and…"

She put her hand up to stop me. "Toni, I cannot believe you would befriend my deceased husband's mistress. Girl, that is the ultimate betrayal."

Jada was pacing back and forth with clenched fists, so I knew my time was short before she completely lost it.

"Listen, we've had a good visit for today, and the kids have enjoyed seeing each other again. Let's not get into this right now, okay? It's time for Lil' Darien's nap, so why don't I get him home and we can talk about this later. Okay?"

At first, she didn't respond. She just stood looking past me as if she was deep in thought. Finally, she came out of her trance.

"Toni, please leave my house now. I need a minute to process everything. I will be in touch with you about seeing my godson on a more regular basis. As for you and I, we'll see. I just need some time to think about everything."

I backed away from her towards the family room where the kids were. Darien was right to be concerned about me forming a friendship with Gina. It never occurred to me that it would cause an issue with Jada and especially since we hadn't been talking. I gathered up Lil' Darien and his things and walked towards the door. Jada didn't follow me. She just stood in the hallway and watched me walk out.

After getting Lil' Darien situated in the car, I sat in the driver's seat for a few moments thinking about what just happened. Putting myself in Jada's shoes, I placed my head on the steering wheel and completely lost it. In between sobs, I asked myself, *How could I have been so stupid?* When there were no more tears left, I composed myself and started up the car. As I drove home, I thought about Jada and Gina and how I could manage to remain friends with both of them without any conflict. Harrisburg was too small for me to sneak around with one without the other one finding out.

Darien would be happy because he never really liked Gina in the first place. He was still angry with her for dogging out Vince like she did. The more I thought about it, the more I realized there was no point in trying to continue anything with Gina. There were too many people in my life that had an issue with our friendship.

Chapter 19

Vince

During the ride, I made small talk with Derrick about school and his friends. He seems like a typical eight-year-old kid. I did notice he kept looking back to make sure Martha was close behind us. I told him about my parents and explained they were waiting for us at my apartment to meet him. As we got closer to the apartment, Derrick began to point out places he knew. When we passed his school, he pointed it out and told me about his friends and his teacher.

After we pulled up to the building, he smiled and asked, "Is this where we are going to live now?"

Smiling, I replied, "Yes. I have an apartment here in this building."

He unbuckled his seat belt. "Wow, this is great. My friend Robbie lives in this building, too, and my mom Martha is right around the corner."

I raised an eyebrow when he said that. I knew his school was close by, but I had no idea Martha lived so close. This was going to be great. I didn't know all of the details surrounding her nasty divorce from her husband, but I did know I was attracted to her. She seemed nice, and clearly, she loved Derrick. I would be happy to have her as a part of his life and even mine for that matter. I had no idea where that thought came from, though. I hadn't been with anyone since Gina and I split, and I hadn't been remotely interested in anyone, except for maybe Jada. Gina hurt me deeply, so I knew it would be awhile before I could open myself up to another woman.

Derrick and I waited for Martha to park, and she met us at the entrance of the building. My mother must have been watching for us, because she met us in the hallway before we reached the door.

When she approached us with her arms outstretched, Derrick turned to me and asked, "Is this my grandma?"

My mother overheard his question and answered for me. "Yes, honey, I am Grandma Evie. Can I get a hug?"

Derrick looked at Martha and I before he agreed, and we both nodded that it was okay. She hugged Derrick for what seemed like hours before letting him go.

The day turned out to be perfect. Derrick and I got along well. My parents loved him, and they liked Martha, too. She stayed for dinner and helped to get Derrick settled into his room for bed. As I walked her to her car, I told her that she was welcome to come and visit Derrick whenever she wanted to. She seemed very pleased that I was so open to her continuing a relationship with him. Truth is, I was interested in getting to know Martha better, as well. She seemed happy most of the time, but at times, I sensed sadness in her and knew there was much more going on with her than losing Derrick.

As I prepared to turn in for the evening, I stopped by Derrick's room and peeked inside. He was sleeping soundly. I headed back towards the guestroom where my parents were and stopped just short of the door. I heard my father say something about Derrick. I inched closer so I could try to make out what they were talking about. I could tell by their tone that it was not a pleasant conversation.

"Evie, I just think Vince should get another test done," I heard my father say. "That boy doesn't look one bit like him."

My mother sucked her teeth and responded, "Victor, we haven't seen that boy's mother. So, maybe he looks like her."

My father's response was, "Well, maybe, but all I know is that boy does not look anything like Vince or any of my people. I just think it's odd the way all of this came about. I simply don't trust it."

There was silence for a few moments, and then I heard my mother say, "Victor, this little boy has been through so much. Can you at least try to be nice to him to make him feel welcome? I understand your concerns, but the courts coordinated the DNA testing and this entire process. So, as far as I'm concerned, everything is legit and that is my grandson lying in the next room sleeping."

I made a noise in the hallway to signal to my parents that I was nearby. Then I lightly tapped on the door, and my mother came to greet me. She smiled at me, while my father turned away. I thought about confronting them about what I had heard, but really wasn't in the mood for anything else today.

I simply said, "I was just coming to let you know I checked on Derrick, and he is sleeping. So, I'm going to turn in for the evening."

My mother smiled at me and gave me a hug. "Dear, we are so proud of you and how you are handling everything." She turned towards my father and said, "Isn't that right, Victor?"

My father cleared his throat and replied, "Oh, yes, son. You are handling things quite well." He then winked at me and added, "I like that Martha girl, too. She seems really nice."

I chuckled, turned around, and simply said, "Goodnight, Mom and Dad. I'll see you in the morning."

Once I retired to my room, I lay awake thinking about the conversation I overheard. Derrick did not resemble me, but I didn't resemble my father either. So, I wasn't going to worry myself about it. The test was done, and the results came back indicating I was his father. I was now Derrick's legal guardian, and we were in the process of getting his birth certificate updated, as well. I did agree with my father's comments about Martha, though. She was nice, and I did intend to keep her around as much as possible.

I had one more day to prepare for starting my new job. I was looking forward to getting into the studio and working on my music. I knew how important it would be to have a structured routine for Derrick to follow in order for him to get used to his new surroundings. Having my mother here for the next few weeks was going to be great. She could help with his before and afterschool care until I established what my work schedule would be. I also planned to sit down with Martha to determine what she would be willing to do to assist with caring for Derrick. I had investigated some afterschool programs. However, I would prefer him to be with her, if she was available. My mind continued to race as I drifted off to sleep, thinking about all of the decisions I would have to make now on behalf of my son.

Victoria

I was on the plane on my way back home from Chicago. I've been spending most of my time in Chicago over the past month working with Rhonda and her connections, confirming the information that we gathered about David, Sr., and validating the sources.

When I started all of this, I had no idea how far reaching this scandal would be. As it turns out, once we reviewed everything we had and the information and sources were verified, the local authorities called in the feds. The feds are taking over, and they will be launching a full investigation of all David, Sr.'s cases. Rhonda and I are concerned about our safety, but we have been assured that once David and his attorneys are made aware of the charges being brought against him, we will be able to seek protective custody. We're not only concerned about David trying to retaliate, but some of the people involved in the cases are very influential, as well. When the truth finally comes out, there are going to be a lot of unhappy people all across the country. I am so glad Jr. is not around to see any of this. He knew his father was into some shady dealings, but he had no idea how deep all of this went. He would be devastated.

I switched positions in my seat and shook my head while thinking about all of the lives that were about to be forever changed because of the unscrupulous dealings of one selfish man. Once I got back home, I had some decisions to make about my future. Ever since David's death, I have been on a mission to seek revenge, and now that I had accomplished my goal, it was time to move on with my life. I had to decide what that meant for me.

For years, I held out hope that David and I would end up together, and now that he is gone, I have to learn how to open up and love again. Yes, I've been seeing Randy for a while now, but really, that was a relationship of convenience; there is no future in it. It's time for me to break things off with him. I knew it would be hard breaking up with him because he felt very deeply for me.

As I drifted off to sleep, I thought back to all of the happy times David, Jr. and I had together, and I wondered if I would ever feel that way again.

Toni

When Darien arrived home, I had dinner prepared and was ready to discuss my Gina/Jada dilemma with him. As I expected, he had no sympathy for me. He listened patiently while I explained everything that happened at Toni's house earlier. Once I finished, he finally decided to respond.

He put his fork down, cleared his throat and said, "Toni, I told you before that I didn't think it was a good idea for you to become friends with Gina."

"I know, babe, but Gina is a nice girl. What is it about her besides what happened between her and Vince that has you so worked up?"

He let out a heavy sigh, and then reached across the table to grab my hand.

"What is it, Darien? Did you use to date her or something?"

He chucked. "No way would I ever date someone like Gina."

I was confused by the way he emphasized the words *someone* and *like*.

"What do you mean, Darien? What do you know about Gina that you're not sharing with me?"

"Okay, Toni, back in the day right after college, when I would come home to visit Mama D and Joy, I would sometimes hang out at the strip club with the boys. I know Gina from the strip club because she use to work there."

"What do you mean work there? You mean as a waitress?"

He shook his head. "No, Toni, she was a stripper."

I couldn't believe it.

"Why in the world would Vince date an ex-stripper? Wait! Did he meet her there?"

He shook his head and said, "No, he didn't. Vince never liked going to strip clubs, and he doesn't know she use to be one either."

"Wow, Darien, that's deep. How could you keep something like that from him?"

He let go of my hand and sat back in his chair with a surprised look on his face.

"I know you're not going to lecture me about keeping secrets from friends, are you?"

His remark could have upset me, but he was right. So, I simply said, "No, I didn't mean it like that. I guess it's just that I'm surprised you didn't mention anything to Vince about it once you recognized her."

He picked up his fork, picked at his food a little bit, and shook his head.

"Toni, trust me, I struggled with that one for a long time. By the time I met Gina, Vince was head over heels in love with her. It was too late. I tried to ask how much he knew about her background and things like that, but he was blinded by love."

"Wow, that's deep. Well, I understand much better now why you had concerns, and I will have to decide how to handle this thing with Gina and Jada. My goal is to work on repairing things with Jada."

Darien smiled and nodded in agreement while continuing to eat his dinner.

I thought about how to let Gina know that we needed to back off of our friendship. It was such a shame because I really liked her.

Chapter 20

Six Months Later
Vince

My alarm went off, and I rolled over to turn it off. Then I rolled back over, closed my eyes, and smiled to myself. I thought about how much my life had changed in the past year. My music career was taking off, and I was raising my eight-year-old son who I just met six months ago. Derrick had adjusted nicely to our living arrangements, and I needed to make a decision as to where we would be living on a permanent basis. My initial plan was to live here in Chicago for the first six months so Derrick and I could get to know each other while he remained in familiar surroundings. Being so far away from my parents was tough. Even though they visited as often as they could, they had their own lives to life and a house that was paid for in Harrisburg. The last time they were here, they mentioned possibly selling their house and moving out here to be closer to Derrick and me. It was a nice gesture, but I really didn't feel comfortable with them making such a major lifestyle change for me. With my music, I needed to remain flexible and able to move around, so I wanted my parents to remain in Harrisburg.

My project with Greg was nearing its end, and he was working on getting me some work that would take me back east for a few months anyway. I told my parents to hold off until we see where I end up.

I heard the bathroom door open and close, which meant Derrick was awake. I looked over at the clock and was surprised to see I had been lying in the bed thinking for so long. I had to get up and get moving, or I was going to be late. I reached for my cell phone and sent the text message that I have been sending every morning for the past few months. I smiled as I hit the send button because I knew the smile that would be on her face when she read it.

David Sr.

I sat in my office looking out over the Baltimore Harbor and sipping my coffee while thinking about Jada and the kids. It's been over seven months since I've seen or talked to them. Jada has been very stubborn and has continued to refuse to accept my calls. I have tried to reach out to her at least once a week over the past several months.

I have been spending a lot of time in Harrisburg visiting and getting to know Samantha and Gina. I've been showering Samantha with gifts and trying to put the pain of losing my son and his oldest children behind me. I have driven past the house on a number of occasions in hopes that I could catch Jada or the kids outside. Each time, the house looked dark and cold, which is exactly how I felt each time I left. I know all of this is my fault, and I really wish there was something I could do to right this wrong.

I turned around to refocus and get back to work on reading the deposition notes from my latest case. Just as I started to make some notes, Lisa buzzed me on the intercom.

"Sir, Jack is on line one for you."

I moved over so I could reach the speakerphone button and pressed it.

"Jack, how are you, buddy?"

There was a heavy sigh and then a moment of silence. I had known Jack for a long time; we used to practice together until we decided it was best to part ways. We decided it would be best to build separate practices, and we listed each other as our legal counsel.

Finally, Jack said, "David, turn on the TV to CNN."

I searched my desk for the remote to the TV and then spotted it across the room on the couch. While walking over towards the couch, I asked, "Jack, what's going on? You sound so somber."

Jack sighed heavily again. "David, it's really bad. I'm not sure I can…"

Just then, the TV came on, and I saw my face plastered all over the screen. I turned the volume up so I could hear, and at the same time in the background, I heard Jack finish his thought, "…help you out of this one. David, they said the feds are involved and that they have dozens of credible witnesses."

My mouth fell open, and I slowly backed towards my couch to sit down. I heard Jack trying to talk to me faintly in the background, but my attention was focused on the TV. The commentator said, "…dozens of counts of witness tampering," and then my heart sunk when I saw the video of First Rate Lab and several employees being taken out in handcuffs. Just then, Lisa cracked open the door and interrupted my thoughts.

She looked at the TV, then back to me and said, "Um, sir, you have several calls on hold, and there are reporters in the lobby, as well."

I didn't move or respond for at least a minute. Lisa walked into my office and closed the door behind her. Then she walked over to me and put her hand on my shoulder.

"Sir, are you okay? What should I do about the calls and the reporters outside?"

I looked up at her, but couldn't make any sound come out of my mouth. I felt like I couldn't breathe. When I heard Jack's voice, I remembered he was on the phone.

"Lisa, call security and have them remove the reporters from the building," Jack told her. "Hold all calls. If the press calls, let them know we will not be making any statements today. Let them know David's legal counsel will contact them tomorrow and provide a formal statement."

Lisa looked at me and asked again, "Sir, are you okay?"

This time, I managed to nod my head yes. She turned and walked towards the door, but she kept looking back at me. Next, I heard Jack's voice again.

"David, are you still there?"

I stood up and walked towards my desk. After picking up the phone's receiver, I replied, "Yes, Jack, I'm still here. What's going on? How did this happen?"

"I have no idea, David, but I can tell you they have a lot of information. This is going to be a tough one to beat. Listen, I'm out of town right now in Atlanta, but I'm going to get on the next flight I can either late tonight or first thing in the morning. Until I get there, don't talk to anyone."

I nodded my head yes, but didn't say anything as I was still processing everything. My flight or fight instinct was kicking into high gear. All sorts of thoughts were going through my head. I even considered fleeing the country.

"David, did you hear me?"

I snapped out of my trance and answered, "Yes, Jack, I heard you, and I understand. Call me when you arrive, and then we can decide where to meet. I have a feeling the press is going to be at my house, too."

"Yes, we should meet somewhere else, but I'm not sure where. Let me go and get my flight reservations taken care of, and I will be in touch."

The line went dead, and I spun my chair around to look out over the harbor again. I couldn't believe this was happening to me. I had been so careful or so I thought. Again, I weighed my options, but as I was considering them, I heard every word being said about me on CNN. I knew this was an impossible situation. There was only one way to handle it. I was so lost in my own thoughts that I didn't hear Lisa come into my office until she was standing right beside me.

"Sir, I had security take care of the reporters that were here, and I am holding all of your calls. Is there anything else I can do for you right now?"

I thought for a minute and then turned towards her. "No, Lisa, there is nothing you can do for me."

I could see the worry in her eyes; she looked as if she was in pain.

Reaching out, I grabbed her hand and said, "Lisa, I'm okay, and I'm going to be okay. Why don't you go ahead and leave for the day? And remember, don't say anything to any reporters or anyone who approaches you."

Lisa started to cry as she shook her head to let me know she understood.

"Go home and stay there until I contact you. Don't worry about coming into work. I will be in touch…and, Lisa, everything is going to be just fine. I assure you."

Lisa wiped the tears from her eyes and said, "I understand, sir, and please, if there is anything you need, do not hesitate to contact me."

She leaned in to hug me, then turned and walked toward the door.

Right before she reached the door, I said, "Lisa, there is one more thing you can do for me."

She turned around and took a few steps back towards me.

"On your way out, please let the security guards know not to let anyone in the parking lot or building today except for Benjamin. Ask them to request that he show his ID to confirm his identity."

She nodded her head, indicating she understood, then turned and headed out the door. After Lisa left, I turned back towards the harbor and continued to contemplate my options. The TV was a distraction, so I raised the remote up to turn it off. I then closed my eyes and enjoyed the silence for a few moments. I realized what I had to do. There were several people that I needed to get in touch with before the news spread; first on my list was Benjamin. I turned around towards my desk, picked up the phone, and dialed his cell phone number. He answered on the third ring sounding a little out of breath.

"Hello, sir…I mean David, Sr.," he said. "How can I help you?"

I switched the phone to my other ear. "Benjamin, where are you right now?"

Sensing the panic in my voice, he replied, "Sir, what's wrong?"

Clearly, he had not been near a television in the past hour or so. I ignored his question and said, "Benjamin, I need to speak with you as soon as possible. How soon can you get here?"

"I can be there within the hour, sir," he responded. "Are you sure you're okay?"

I was relieved that he was local and could get to me soon.

"Benjamin, get here as soon as you can, and please do me a favor. Don't talk to anyone. Just get in your car and come straight here. Don't stop anywhere."

Benjamin responded, "Okay, sir. I am on my way now."

I disconnected the call, got up, and walked over to the door. I cracked it open to confirm that Lisa was gone and that no one else was there. All was quiet in the lobby. So, I closed my door back and locked it. Next, I headed over to my bookcase, grabbed the book, took it over to my desk, and sat down. I opened the book, reached in, took the gun out, and laid it on my desk. I stared at it for a long while. Then I picked up the gun and checked to see how many bullets were in it. My hand was shaking as I placed the gun back down on my desk. I looked around my office at all of my diplomas and awards. I also took notice of all the pictures of David, Jr. and my grandchildren. I had worked so hard to keep my family safe and secure, but it seemed as if everything had taken a turn for the worse. Since the day David, Jr. died, my life hasn't been the same. I reached in my drawer for a notepad and started writing.

Benjamin

When Sr. called, I was just leaving the gym. I had gone there to work out during my lunch hour. Since I had dinner plans tonight, I knew I wouldn't be able to get my workout in after work. Traffic should not be too bad since it was just past one o'clock and most of the lunch traffic had died down. David, Sr. sounded very stressed and upset. My thoughts were racing all over the place as I wondered what could have him so upset. Since the night at Jada's house, he and I had very little contact. I reached out to him at least once a month, but usually I got his voicemail or spoke to Lisa, who filled me in on the fact that he had been spending a lot of time in Harrisburg with Samantha and Gina. As I merged onto Interstate 495, I realized I had underestimated what traffic would be like. It appeared to be backed up. Unless things opened up quickly, I would not make it to David, Sr.'s office within the hour like I had promised. Knowing how much he hated when someone wasn't on time, I thought about calling him, but decided to just wait it out and see how long it took me to make it into the city.

Chapter 21

Jada

Everyone woke up late this morning, so it was past lunchtime and I was just getting a chance to check my personal cell phone for messages. I had missed my daily morning message and was awaiting confirmation about my dinner plans for tonight. Every morning, I awoke to the sound of my cell phone chirping, letting me know I had a text message. I didn't even have to look at it to know who it was from. This had become our ritual. I didn't even need an alarm clock anymore. Well, maybe I did since I completely missed it this morning and ended up being late for work.

First thing in the morning, I would receive a "Good morning, sunshine" text from him. I picked up my phone and looked at my messages to confirm my morning message was indeed waiting for me. I smiled as I always did when I received the message from him. I wasn't sure where any of this was headed, but I was enjoying the attention, and having someone who thought of me every day was nice.

My thoughts were quickly interrupted by my assistant, who let me know my next meeting was about to start. I put my phone down, gathered my notepad, and headed towards the conference room. Things had really picked up at the office the past few months. We were launching a new product, and there was so much work to do. Most days once I got to the office, it was non-stop until it was time to go home.

Toni's replacement was still getting up to speed. I had to admit I really missed her around here. We've been talking more and have had a few girls' night out dinners over the past few months, but I still wasn't ready to go back to the way things had been before.

Toni

I emailed Jada to confirm I could take Lil' Darien over to her place tonight for a sleepover. Darien had to leave early for a business trip tomorrow, and since his car was in the shop, I needed to drive him to the airport at four o'clock in the morning. Lil' Darien was finally on somewhat of a schedule, and I didn't want to have to drag him out at that time of morning. I'm spoiled with having Joy around to help at times like this, but she was sleeping over at a friend's house tonight. So, Jada was my only option.

It has been seven months since the night Jada called everyone out about the secrets and lies they were keeping from everyone else. Even though I had slowly distanced myself from Gina, things were still not back to normal between us. It took Jada a month or so after the lunch at her house to answer my calls again. Once she did, we met again, and I explained that I was no longer friends with Gina and told her why. We agreed to get back to our monthly girls' night out dinners, and she also wanted to have Lil' Darien over one weekend a month to give Darien and me a break. I welcomed the break and offered to do the same for her. I knew Jada well, and I sensed she was still holding back and not sharing something with me. I decided we were both just a little gun-shy because of all the secrets and lies we had held and told each other over the past few years. It was going to take some time for us to gain each other's trust back fully.

One subject that was difficult for us to discuss was Benjamin. It was hard for me to discuss how I felt about him openly since I read the letter, and it seemed that Jada had completely changed her perception of him. She went from having complete hatred of him to constantly saying how wonderful he was and that he was her hero. She often asked me how I knew Darien was the one for me after being so madly in love with Benjamin all those years. It was a tough question for me to answer, and that bothered me because I remember a time when I could talk for hours about Darien and how special he was to me.

I miss the way our friendship was before, but I know she's still upset with me. I often ask myself if I would do anything differently knowing what I know now about the situation with David, Jr. Would I still keep the truth from Jada? The answer is probably yes. I still felt that after his death, what good was it for her to know what he did seven years prior? The same thing applies to the situation with Gina. I still don't feel she needed to know that. What good would it have done? I guess maybe if I had known about Samantha, I might have thought Jada should know about their affair.

Darien got a promotion at work and has been traveling more frequently. With his raise, I am able to stay home full time, which I love. I spend time with Lil' Darien, manage the rental property affairs, and have been spending a lot more time writing. I have even contemplated writing a book. Darien has been supportive about everything. Joy is settled into her new routine of living with us and is actually doing well in school.

I finally met Derrick. Vince brought him to Harrisburg soon after he won custody, and it was nice to meet my son after so many years. Darien handled it much better than I thought he would. I try to keep in touch with him via email, and we also Skype several times a week. Derrick is adjusting nicely to his new living arrangements, and he really seems to be taking to Vince. Vince's parents were also being supportive and had been spending a lot of time in Chicago helping him out. Vince was unsure about moving back to Harrisburg with Derrick, and I had mixed emotions about it. I felt the constant reminder of seeing Vince,

Derrick, and I together might cause problems for Darien. Darien and I are settled into a nice rhythm now, and I don't want to do anything to upset our relationship.

I never thought I would be a stay-at-home mom or housewife, but I am settling in to my new role quite nicely. This isn't quite the life I imagined when I used to dream about my future with Benjamin, but this is good. Things could not be any better. Well, if Jada and I were on better terms, it would be better. I know she just needs more time. Eventually she will come around and things will be back to the way they used to be. Actually, I guess things will never be back to the way they used to be since David is gone and Benjamin and I are not together. All this time, I had been hoping things could return to normal or the way they had been before. It finally hit me that things will never be that way again, and the realization made me a little melancholy.

I had been sitting at the computer much longer than I realized. I was startled from my thoughts by my computer announcing I had a new email. I checked, and it was from Jada. She confirmed that she could take Lil' Darien tonight. She said she had plans for dinner, but would pick him up on her way home. That was perfect. I responded, signed out of my email account, and went upstairs to check on Lil' Darien.

David, Sr.

I put the final touches on my letters, sealed them all, and put them on my desk. All except for the one for Benjamin. I took his letter and grabbed a piece of tape. I got up from my desk, walked over to the door, and put my ear against it to make sure I didn't hear any movement outside the door. Once I felt comfortable there was no one on the other side, I quickly opened the door and taped his letter to it. Then I closed and locked the door and headed back towards my desk.

I grabbed the remote and turned the TV back on before sitting down. I glanced over at the clock on my desk and realized Benjamin should be arriving soon. I turned my attention back to the TV, and as I feared, they were still talking about me. The video of the workers from the lab leaving the building in handcuffs continued to play, and the reporters were giving up-to-the-minute updates on all the information they had gathered.

I turned around in my chair and looked out at the harbor for what might be the last time. I loved this view. I thought back to all of the times David, Jr. and I had stood at this window looking out over the harbor and talking about the plans for the future. I thought about what I had written in the letter to Jada and Gina. They were going to be hearing some awful things about me in the media, and I had to give them my side of the story. Benjamin's letter took the longest to write. I included details in his letter that only I knew, and I gave him instructions that I knew I could trust him to follow.

I sat and waited for Benjamin to arrive.

Benjamin

When I arrived at Sr.'s office, I immediately noticed a crowd of people standing around. I also saw the security guards and some police trying to keep the crowd under control. The entrance to the parking lot was blocked, and when I approached, a security guard came over to my car.

When I rolled the window down, he said, "Sorry, sir, but we have strict orders not to let anyone in the building."

Confused, I wondered what was going on. I finally said, "Mr. Wright just called me about an hour ago and told me to come right over to meet with him."

He bent down, looked at me, and asked, "What is your name, sir?"

"My name is Benjamin Royal," I responded.

"Mr. Royal, can I see some ID please?"

I unfastened my seatbelt and reached into my pocket to pull out my wallet. I removed my driver's license and handed it to the guard. He took it from my hand, checked my name, then turned and motioned to his partner to let me through.

195

He handed my license back to me and said, "Go on through, sir. Park right by the entrance and another guard will escort you to the elevator once you are inside of the building."

I was getting very concerned now, but fought the urge to ask questions. I put my license back into my wallet and pulled into the parking space right by the door as the guard instructed, even though it was a handicap space. I barely had the car in park before I opened the door to get out. I sprinted to the door, and as the first guard said, there was a guard waiting to let me in the building.

As we walked towards the elevator, I couldn't take it anymore, so I asked, "Excuse me, sir, but what's going on?"

He shook his head and said, "I really don't know all the details, sir, but some major story broke earlier this afternoon about Mr. Wright, and ever since then this place has been swarming with reporters."

Just then, the elevator doors opened and he motioned for me to step inside. I stepped in, thanked the guard, and pushed the button. When the doors closed, I stepped back and leaned against the wall of the elevator. I had no idea what was going on, but I had a bad feeling about it.

When the doors opened, I quickly stepped out of the elevator and looked around. There was no one there. The office was completely empty. I walked towards Sr.'s office. The door was closed, but there was something taped to it. As I approached, I could hear the TV on in his office, and I was surprised to see the note had my name on it. I reached for the envelope and removed it from the door. At the same time, I knocked on the door and waited, but there was no response. I tried to open the door, but it was locked. I stepped back and looked around, dazed and confused. I knocked on the door again, waited, and heard nothing except for the TV. Finally, I walked back towards the reception area, sat down, and opened the envelope. The handwritten letter read:

Dear Benjamin,

Please make sure Jada and Gina receive their letters that I left on my desk. As soon as you can, get in contact with Jack. He is my attorney, and he will handle everything from here. He knows where all of my important papers are, such as my will. He also has access to my safety deposit box, which contains some additional papers that will be important to you and the others.

I could give you many sorry excuses for why I did the things I did, but the simple fact is that none of it matters. You spent seven years in jail for a crime you did not commit because I could not bear the thought of my son being behind bars for one minute, let alone seven years. Maybe one day when your son is grown, you will understand how it feels to love someone that much. Benjamin, Toni's son that she gave up is your son. I paid someone off at the lab to switch the results. I know it does not mean much at this point, but I am truly sorry.
David

I read and re-read the letter at least three times before it sank in. I experienced every emotion possible in the span of a few seconds. I was in shock, angry, happy, but the last emotion was rage. I stood up, headed towards Sr.'s door, and started banging on it while screaming his name.

"David, open this door right now and face me, damn it!"

I listened and heard nothing but the TV. So, I started banging on the door again. Then I heard it—a gunshot—and I instinctively dropped to the floor, where I stayed for a few minutes not moving. I heard a thud, and it sounded like it came from Sr.'s office. Once I felt safe, I slowly got up and looked around. I didn't see anyone. That's when I realized the gunshot came from inside Sr.'s office. I tried the door again, but it was still locked. So, I stepped back and kicked the door as hard as I could, and it flew open. I was not prepared for what I saw next.

David, Sr. was laying facedown on his desk, blood spatter and brain matter all over his window. I slowly backed out of his office, and once I was in the lobby, I turned around and sprinted to the elevator. I pushed the button, and when the doors opened, the security guard was standing inside with his gun drawn. I immediately put my hands up and started to back away. Tears were streaming down my cheeks as I motioned towards Sr.'s office without saying a word.

The guard walked past me, and with his gun still pointed at me, he said, "Get down on the ground and put your hands behind your back."

I did exactly as he said. I knew I hadn't done anything wrong, and I had seen too many people get hurt while trying to plead their cases to the guards in jail. So, I stayed down on the ground as he walked over towards the office. Once he saw David, Sr., he gasped and immediately radioed down to his partner to send the police officer upstairs. Then he walked back towards me.

"Get up on your feet. What happened up here, sir? Did you find him this way when you got up here?"

I shook my head yes and started to explain exactly what happened, but was interrupted by the other guard and police coming off the elevator.

After several hours of police questioning and giving my statement to at least a half dozen people, I was finally on my way headed north on Interstate 83. I had two important stops to make. First, I had to visit Jada to break the news to her about David, Sr. and to deliver her letter. I knew she was concerned when I missed our dinner date for tonight. Once the police finally released me, I checked my phone and she had left several messages and sent a few texts. I felt bad about how things were going to end up, but things have changed now. I think we were both vulnerable and hurting, which is why we were drawn to each other. We've been talking and seeing each other for the past few months now. Thank goodness we never slept together, although I felt we were getting close the last time I saw her.

After I dealt with Jada, I was going to Toni's house to tell her that Derrick is my son and then let the chips fall where they may. I was taking a big risk, but I felt this connection, us having a child together, would bring her back to me.

Toni

Jada picked up Lil' Darien a little earlier than expected. She said her plans for the evening had changed. Having already dropped Joy off at her friend's house for the sleepover, I was happy for the extra time to make sure Darien's bag was packed for his business trip in the morning. He would be going to Florida for a few days.

Chapter 22

Victor

I had just come from the kitchen, where I had fixed myself a nice sized piece of Evie's homemade apple cobbler. I settled in to watch the news, while Evie sat in her chair working on one of her needlepoint projects. We talked to Vince and Derrick earlier, and we were both looking forward to our trip to visit them in a few days. I had to admit I had been very skeptical about Vince taking on this challenge of raising a child on his own, but he had made me proud. The news started with all the normal stuff—kids vandalizing cars and mugging people downtown. I shook my head and took my first bite of the cobbler. Then the news anchor said something that caught both of our attention.

BREAKING NEWS out of Chicago tonight where several employees of First Rate Laboratory have been arrested today on charges of DNA test tampering.

My jaw dropped and so did my fork. I turned to look at Evie, who had stopped in mid stitch and was staring at the TV with her mouth open.

Finally finding my composure, I said, "Evie, did you hear that?"

"Yes, I did," she responded. "Are you thinking what I'm thinking?"

Darien

I sat down on the couch and turned to the news. Toni was upstairs checking my bag to make sure I had everything I needed for my trip. I had missed the first few minutes, but was just in time to hear the lead in for the breaking news story from Chicago. I listened, and just when I was about to call for Toni, I heard the doorbell ring. I looked at my cell to confirm it was way too late for anyone to be ringing my doorbell. I grabbed the remote to record the news so I could come back and listen to the story later, and then I headed towards the door.

I heard Toni at the top of the steps asking, "Who's at the door, babe?"

"I have no idea who would be here this late at night," I responded.

I opened the door and there stood Benjamin looking like he had literally ran from Maryland to our house.

"Where is Toni?" Benjamin asked, pushing past me.

To say I was irritated would be an understatement. I closed the door, walked up to him, and said, "Yo, man, why are you disrespecting me and my house barging in here this time of night like this?"

He seemed to be out of breath as he threw his hands up. "Look, man, I'm sorry, but I have to see Toni right away. Something terrible has happened."

Just then, Toni came around the corner. "Babe, who's at the…" Her voice trailed off once she looked up and saw Benjamin standing there.

Benjamin stepped towards her, and I instinctively moved towards her, as well.

"Toni, something terrible has happened, and I have to talk to you."

She looked at me, and I knew she was waiting for my reaction. I took a step towards Benjamin to place myself in between him and Toni.

"Benjamin, whatever it is you're going to have to sit down and talk to the both of us at the same time. Toni and I don't have any secrets."

"Yes, of course," Benjamin replied. "I understand, but can we please sit down so I can explain?"

As Toni started towards the family room, Benjamin followed her. Toni sat down on the sofa and motioned for Benjamin to sit on the chair across from where she was sitting. I grabbed the remote, turned the TV off, and sat down on the other side of Toni. After Benjamin collected his thoughts, he started to explain.

"Toni and Darien, I am sorry to barge in on you both like this unannounced, but something terrible has happened."

Toni started to fidget in her seat. "Benjamin, you keep saying that. What is it?"

Benjamin lowered his head, took a deep breath, then reached into his pocket and took out a piece of paper. He handed it to Toni. She reached for the paper, opened it, and we both started to read it. We got to the part about the baby at the same time, and Toni screamed and clutched her chest.

Jumping up, I yelled, "Benjamin, where in the hell did you get this letter? Why are you coming into my house bringing all this drama?"

Toni grabbed my arm and said, "Babe, calm down. Let Benjamin tell us what is going on."

When I turned and looked into Toni's eyes, I immediately regained my composure and sat back down. I nodded to Benjamin to continue. Benjamin started at the beginning, telling us about the scandal with the DNA lab and the allegations of witness tampering on other cases. Then he told us about David, Sr. killing himself and leaving the letter for Benjamin admitting that he had someone tamper with the DNA results. He didn't give a full explanation in his letter to Benjamin as to why, but he did in the letter he wrote to Jada. In Jada's letter, David, Sr. explained that it was his final attempt to keep Toni and Benjamin apart so the truth about David would not come out. In the middle of Benjamin's explanation, it occurred to Toni that Jada did not know about David, Sr.'s suicide.

She stopped Benjamin and said, "I have to go to Jada. She is going to be very upset to hear about David, Sr."

Shaking his head no, Benjamin told her, "Jada already knows, Toni. I stopped at her house first. I wanted her to come over here with me, but she couldn't since Lil' Darien was there and she didn't feel up to getting all the kids out of bed. She was in quite a bit of shock after hearing about Sr., so I decided to come over here alone."

Toni looked from Benjamin to me and then said, "Babe, I have to go and see about Jada, and I have to go get Lil' Darien."

I stood up. "Toni, do you know what time it is?"

Toni reached for my arm. "Yes, babe, I know it's late, but I have to go to Jada. She needs me. Can't you understand that?"

I was fuming, but I knew there was nothing I could say to make her stay. As I sat back down on the couch, Toni got up and went upstairs to get her shoes and purse. While she was gone, I took the opportunity of being alone with Benjamin to set some ground rules with him. I moved forward in my seat so I could speak directly to him without raising my voice.

"Benjamin, I understand how much of a shock it must be to find out that the baby Toni gave up was actually yours, but I just want to remind you that Toni is my wife now and we also have a son together. Just because that child is yours doesn't mean you and Toni are going to get back together. I love that woman more than life itself, and I will not stand by and watch you try to take my wife away from me."

I heard Toni coming back down the stairs, so I put my finger to my lips to motion to Benjamin to be quiet and not respond right now.

When Toni came back into the room, she looked from me to Benjamin and then said, "Okay, Benjamin, I'm ready to go."

As she walked over to me, I stood up, and she gave me a hug and a kiss. I knew her actions were to make sure I knew that she loved me and that I had nothing to worry about.

Toni

I followed Benjamin outside to his car. He opened the door and I got in. As I sat waiting for him to get in and start the car, my mind was racing. My emotions were all over the place. I looked back towards the house and could see Darien standing in the window watching. A single tear fell from my eye as I watched him. I was sad that things had turned out this way. I felt a sense of relief knowing that Derrick was Benjamin's son. I always felt it, but when the test came back saying it was Vince's, it never occurred to me that the test was wrong. Never in a million years would I have thought David, Sr. would have paid someone to tamper with the results.

All those years I waited for Benjamin I knew there was a bond between us. Jada always made me feel like I was crazy for having such faith and confidence in our love. Once I read the letter he wrote to me while he was in jail, I knew we had to be together again. It was just a matter of time.

Benjamin got in and started the car. Then he turned to me and asked, "Where to?"

I faced him and replied, "Jada's house. I have to pick up Lil' Darien."

Benjamin looked disappointed in my response as he turned away from me and put the car in drive.

"And then to Chicago," I continued. "We have to go there so you can meet our son. Then we can go wherever you want to. Just as long as we're together I will be happy."

Benjamin turned and smiled at me before pulling away from my house. I looked back one last time at the life I had built and was running away from.

THE END

Today's Truth

Discussion Questions

1. Would you tell your best friend that their spouse was cheating if you found out he or she was?
2. How would you feel if you found out after their death that your spouse had been unfaithful?
3. What character was your favorite and why?
4. Which character do you feel had the most impact on the story?
5. Do you feel it was wrong for Jada to read the letters Benjamin wrote to Toni?
6. Which character was your least favorite and why?
7. Do you think Toni was wrong for becoming friends with Gina?
8. How did you feel about how Darien handled things with Vince?
9. What was the most shocking thing in the book?
10. Do you think that Toni is really in love with Darien?
11. Do you think that Benjamin was wrong to trust David Sr. to handle the paternity testing results?
12. Do you feel Jada should allow her kids to meet Samantha? Why or why not?
13. Have you ever kept a journal? If so what types of things did you write about?
14. An overall thought on the book and the authors writing style.